M.H. Williams graduated in English Literature, and from the very beginning of her childhood she was in love with poetry and literature. Her biggest dream was to write a book about her concern about the modern people of her country whose lives are in the hands of the totalitarian Leader. She seeks to pour her muted and repressed voice into this book in order to be heard by the world. Her book depicts the cold war between people and the totalitarian regime.

I have to express my gratitude to my parents and my little sister because of their constant support and without them I have never been able to publish this book. I have to show my respect to those who stand against our repressive government and sacrifice themselves for us. This book is a dedication to all those lost voices whose constant efforts for making a better country have been underestimated. For Woman, Life, Freedom…

M.H. Williams

Notes from a Restricted Land

Austin Macauley Publishers™
London • Cambridge • New York • Sharjah

A CIP catalogue record for this title is available from the British Library.

ISBN 9781398471672 (Paperback)
ISBN 9781398471689 (ePub e-book)

www.austinmacauley.com

First Published 2023
Austin Macauley Publishers Ltd®
1 Canada Square
Canary Wharf
London
E14 5AA

Table of Contents

Note 1
On the Birth of Restricted Land

Have you ever been this weary to write notes about yourself to unknown people? Well, let me answer this for you, no you haven't. I don't even know how should I start. To be honest, I'm scared of opening my heart to strangers who I can't trust. But there must be someone who dares to talk about Restricted land and its dark secrets which has been remained untold for years. As a 26-year-old girl, I have to admit that living in Restricted land is not an easy job. What do you know girls about being a puppet of your society? Letting your government decides for you like you're a robot or their pet psychopath. When the leader of my society instead of helping me, tries to suffocate me, how should I react? Madness has been ruling over years in Restricted land and I condemned to accept it not me but all of us. We don't need a saviour but we need a better society to live. You may think it is a cliché but sometimes I feel my shadow is spying on me so I have to be careful about what I want to do. I wish I knew when I'm going to get rid of this situation. I mean, I know I will but I don't know the exact time. That day will come, I have no doubt about it and then I will become a person who makes her own decisions all by herself. We all have to admit that the interference of the leader in our lives is so annoying. Actually, it is our pet peeve. Now imagine a society in which somebody else thinks since he is your leader, he can give you orders about what you should wear and how you are supposed to behave. Let me tell you something, it seems ridiculous but I was the eyewitness of those worried parents whose daughters were arrested because of mandatory *Hijab*.

I mean, it's a shame when your society imposed its dogmatic opinion on you. You know what I'm saying right? All we need is a freedom of choice but the leader aims to create a society in which people are the copies of his ideal. No matter if his ideal is stupid or not, people have to follow his rules. Being different is not allowed. It is not North Korea. Having *Hijab* is a matter of choice and therefore nobody has the right to give us instructions for having or not having it. I lament the lack of humanity in Restricted land. The dictatorship of our totalitarian leader and its anti-women laws leave no choice for women who prefer not to have *Hijab*. Personally, I think our society could be a better place to live only if our government would let us be ourselves. We all deserve happiness and peace but the problem is that I can't even define what peace and happiness are because of the gloomy atmosphere of our country.

Note 2
On the Limitation of Having Fun

I am a university student and I have to read many books, maybe that is why I can't bear this injustice in Restricted Land. Reading books about American history gives me information about the issue that at least there was one marginalised group who fought against dictatorship and superiority of narrow-minded leaders. Women who sustained their voice in a patriarchal society, black people who fought for their rights, all used to be subordinate to their masters one day. But what about Restricted land? Did we fight for our own rights? Yes, of course, we did. Many people sacrificed themselves but nothing changed. Right now, the only resolution which pops to Restricted landian's minds is to emigrate because they have the rights to be both happy and free. It is a battle of wills between an oppressive government and people and apparently, the government is more powerful than people. In Restricted land, people's enjoyment does limit to eating out, having party, or shopping. But what kind of party? Please, don't laugh, but boys and girls are not supposed to be in the same room because this is against the law of my society. So, if we have a plan to have fun, we have to do it covertly, otherwise bad things will happen. I mean, no one wants to spend a night in jail. And bad things mean, we are going to be surrounded by police just because we wanted to have fun. Having fun is the basic right of human beings but we have been deprived of a normal life because we were born in Restricted land. I'm not exaggerating but people in here are dead inside. They just breathe. Laughing is not allowed. Having fun is forbidden. Standing against the stupid laws will end tragically. Many parents lost their sons or daughters and many children became orphan just because they expressed their discontent with their government and its selfish leader. To cut a long story short, only one egotist leader can destroy his people's lives and then calls himself a saviour. But I'm sure he is not even able to make a distinction between a destroyer and a saviour. The leader of Restricted Land thinks we all are his prisoners so if we rebel, we will die without a doubt. People were born free that's what God says but Restricted landian people are not free maybe because we are not people. Yes, we aren't. Because we are a puppet in the eyes of our leader and our job is to say yes to the present system. We fought for our own rights but it didn't work so we have been forced to adjust ourselves to this lifestyle.

Nope that's not a lifestyle actually, it's better to say it is a dead style. Because technically we're not living but we only pretend. We are good at this. Restricted landian people should be considered as the best actors around the world since we know how to personify a lucky person.

Note 3
On the State of Being an Anonymous Person

It's a third note and yet I don't dare introduce myself. Maybe I have to find a pen name for myself since I live in Restricted land. I love my country. I really do. Sometimes my mum blames me for being a traitor, because I am criticising the government and the leader of Restricted land. But that is who I am. I can't just sit and observe what is happening around me because I read a lot. I mean reading books helps me a lot. I realise that freedom will come from constant effort. By thinking about freedom, we're not going to be a free man. Okay. Where was I? Yeah, I think the subject was about me choosing a pen name. I can't reveal my own identity not because I'm afraid of death but because I do care about my parents and my sister and I don't want to jeopardise their lives. Talking about Restricted land is forbidden. I mean as long as we praise the leader and the government, we're not in a trouble but the point is that I'm not complimenting, I'm trying to open the eyes of the brainwashed people whose eyes must be closed according to the law of Restricted land. What kind of name should I choose? George Eliot number two is fine, I think. What about a nickname? *Les Misérables* suits us. By us I mean Restricted landian people. Joking aside, I think I should choose a name. *Offred* would be fine too. Okay, from now on I will call myself *Offred.* One day I will tell you who am I, but now it is not a good time for revealing my identity.

Note 4
On the Countries

No, definitely today is not a good day. I just had a fight with my mum. She blamed me for writing about Restricted land and she wants me to write about another country. She blamed me for writing against my country. Well, I told her this is my job, and my country is my concern. My mum doesn't know but I know that Fitzgerald didn't write about Restricted land in his masterpiece, *The Great Gatsby*, but America. Toni Morrison's lamentation of slavery in *Beloved* is not about my country either. They were Americans and they had the guts to write about political and social issues of their countries. But my mum can't even listen to what I say because she is one of those brainwashed people who is believing in the present system. I have to tell you, changing her mind is not easy at all. Maybe she doesn't want to accept the truth. The government talks for her and that's the problem. A toxic government will be the result of people's corruption and that is a fact. So many people in Restricted land were infected by the toxic attitudes of our leader and there is almost no chance to help them rebuild themselves. Sometimes I thank God for giving me this opportunity to live in Restricted land not in North Korea. At least, I'm free to choose my own hairstyle. Oh, I just remember that choosing my own hairstyle is not as easy as you think. I've been thinking about shaving my head for years but as a 26-year-old girl I can't even change my hairstyle without my parents' permission.

Finally, I persuade them that if a girl wants to shave her head it does not mean that she is a whore. Yeah, you may think this couldn't be real but unfortunately it is. Judging book by its cover is what we do all the time in this country. It is our favourite hobby. If a girl wears a pair of tight jeans, then she is a whore and she must go to jail for violating the laws of Restricted land; however, embezzlement and bribery are not considered as a crime here. The corruption of Restricted land only depends on women's tight pants and if we do not care about what we're going to wear outside, we will jeopardise the virtue of our community. If you think I'm joking, I have to tell you that you are wrong. This is what this is. No exaggeration. You know why I chose *Offred* as my pen name? Because we, women are under the control of our patriarchal society and we have to act as we're told. But according to my dictionary free will is defined otherwise. I have been silent all these years, observing the cruelty of totalitarian regime in Restricted land but now I shouldn't waste my time anymore. We are human beings, and we deserve to live in peace not only to rest in peace. We've been pursuing happiness in a country which is devoid of any humanity. So, it's our fault since we're looking for something which doesn't even exist here. It's like looking for gold in the pockets of a poor person. The only thing you can find in their pockets is dust. To be honest, I think they must be grateful for having dust in their pocket at least because I know some people who don't even have dust in their pockets. So, what we do is that we leave our hometown and our childhood memories behind because we have the right to not be a slave. Slavery does not only mean working in a mine because you're forced. Slavery could be decision-making of somebody else for you and imposing of his belief on you.

I won't call the head of Restricted land a leader but I want to call him a murderer who kills people's soul in order to be alive. My mum is the victim of this system, so as my father. I can't argue with them since they believe in what is happening around us. They think value is what we wear not how we think. There are many books which we judge by their pretentious cover, but as soon as we open these books, we will realise their contents are inappropriate. In Restricted land, appearances will define who you are not your abilities. That may justify the cause of brain drain of Restricted landian intellects. Why should they waste their life for a society who doesn't even care about them? This society needs wide pants with empty mind for the sake of its survival. So only those who gave their consent to this system are able to live here. There are two major groups who can live here. Those who are blind enough to not see the reality, and those who benefit from the ignorance of people. As long as our government is replete with a bunch of liars, people will never understand what reality is. It's like Ibsen's *A Doll's house*. I mean Nora finds her freedom in leaving her house to embrace her real identity. If she was a beautiful toy to her husband, now she wants to be an independent person who's strong enough to stand against the irrationality of Helmer. Restricted land is a dollhouse as well. Once we escape from this house, we will find our real self. Then we are no longer a puppet but an independent person.

Note 5
On the Universities

Let me begin this note with some memories from the past about being a university student in Restricted land. Literary criticism is one of our courses which we should have passed in order to become familiar with different approaches such as feminism, psychoanalysis, postcolonialism, queer theory, and… But the problem was when we had to take this important course with a narrow-minded teacher. There would be no queer theory then because we live in Restricted land. Reading about LGBTQ is taboo in my country let alone you want to be gay or lesbian. When it comes to feminism, our job is to attack this movement because in Restricted land women are not equal to men. Men are always subject. This is a patriarchal society with misogynistic motto. So, you are either criticise feminism or you'll fail the course. Postcolonialism was my teacher's favourite subject since he was able to talk about England and America, introducing them as criminals who occupied other countries, imposing their own opinion on the third-world people. But there is a question here. Why didn't he notice our wretched situation? We are people too. We all know about Indians. It's time to know about ourselves. There is no community without a problem but our problems originate in the stupidity of most of Restricted landian people and the dishonesty of our system. Men and women are different. This is not what I say, this is what the schools make an effort to teach. Even our books are different. Picture of a girl should not be in the textbooks of a boy and vice versa. Because this would be the beginning of corruption and we may lose the path of virtue. Then boom. What would be the outcome? The outcome is that we are not educated enough to know how we should react when we meet the opposite sex.

I was scared of opposite sex because the only thing my parents and the society taught me was that trusting the opposite sex will have its own consequences which are damaging. When I went to the university for the first time, I did my best to keep my distance from the boys by calling them by their family names and being defensive for no reason. Going home was the worst part of my life. Since I was a university student, I couldn't ask him, my father, to pick me up from the university. Other students would laugh at me. I was mature enough to take a taxi whenever I wanted to go home. I was 18. My dad was no longer able to pick me up from the university and it was my own problem and I had to deal with it. Being in a same car with a stranger! Being in a same car with an opposite sex! That's not going to happen. This is what I said. You can't understand me. It was such a nightmare for me. Every time I took a taxi, I was afraid of sexual harassment. And only God knew that. I was afraid of men because my parents wanted me to be afraid of them. So, the first two years of B.A. had been spent on this issue. Me, being a coward who was not able to have a connection with the opposite sex. But finally, I overcame this stupid fear and I found some good friends. This was when I understood that I shouldn’t have let my parents gave me instructions. My existence is separate from their existence so I have to think by myself.

Note 6
On the Equality

My mum asked me that why am I writing about something which everybody knew already. She wants me to say something new. 'If people are aware of the situation, then why they are still ignorant. You know what? People in here are careless about what is happening around them. The government persuades them to be thankful for what they have,' I told her.

If somebody has only one pair of shoes, he must be thankful because there are some people in Africa whose feet are bare. If we have food to eat, there are some countries around the world whose people passed away because of hunger. But I wonder how the heads of our society are living in their mansions and they become richer every year. Inflation only changes our lives not theirs. I can't understand how! But math could be tricky sometimes! Oh, I almost forgot what is going on in here? It is because 'Some animals are equal, but some animals are more equals than others.' Thank you, Mr Orwell for reminding me what is happening in Restricted land. Our pigs love bossing around us. I wish I could find an opportunity to kill them all. But no, I'm not a murderer, I want peace. And blood means violence. Who am I? I would never be able to hurt someone's feeling, let alone killing people. I sometimes break some hearts but then I give my best shot in order to be forgiven. I know I talk too much. But since there is nobody here to listen, I have to write. Words will be gone one day. But this book will remain even if I die. Well, if I want to tell you the truth, 20 years ago life was more bearable here. But right now, everybody's resolution for escaping from problems is to leave Restricted land. I think this would be a good decision only if our plane wasn't shot down shortly after its take-off, unintentionally or intentionally. Even the sky of Restricted land would jeopardise our lives. You may not understand the reference. But that's okay it is all about a specific flight which was shot by the Restricted landian guards. And if it helps, I have to tell you that, in that flight we lost so many geniuses whose country didn't give them the attention they deserved. Okay, I think that's enough. I don't even know why I spill the beans, I was supposed to keep the secret of Restricted land to myself without sharing it to anybody else.

Note 7
On the Personal Life of the Author

Another note from Restricted land and nothing have changed. I haven't told you about my first crush? Have I? Don't laugh, please. You shouldn't have expected too much from a girl who has been warned about men. My first crush was one of my university professors when I was 19 or 20. Actually, I fell in love with a married man. Don't judge me. I was immature and he was so good to me. So, my first impression of him was that he is definitely in love with me. How was I supposed to know? Before that I used to be surrounded by girls. I wasn't even as friendly as I was supposed to be with my cousins. So, this was my understanding, if somebody is kind to me, it means he loves me. It was my man-made fact. I was 20 years old but my perception of things was lame. That was not my fault. Because I'd never seen a guy be this kind and adorable in my eyes and I thought it must be something. I didn't tell him that I like him because I'm not a bitch. I couldn't ruin his life just because of my unstable feelings for him. All I could do was to take part in his class although I was done with his course and I passed the course successfully. I took photos of him, sharing my feelings with my parents but they believed that this feeling is not serious so it would be gone soon because it was based on nothing. They were right. The feeling was gone. And now, I still don't know why I fell in love with a man twice my age. But funny enough, I made the same mistake again. Yeah, I really did.

Another teacher, but this time in an English institution. I thought he was the one. My day and night were summarised in thinking about him. I couldn't sleep. I couldn't think. I just wanted him to be mine. I don't know where he is now. And I don't want to talk about him anymore. He was a handsome man whose voice was enough to make me fall in love with him. He was kind to me and he flirted with me a lot. That was another stage of knowing the opposite sex. I was stupid enough to think that if someone is flirting with me, it means that he loves me. All of these mistakes are originated in keeping my distance from the opposite sex. That's my parents' fault. Keeping my distance from the opposite sex didn't help me at all but I understood how weak I was towards men. Every single attention from a guy for me was a sign of love. And I hated myself for being this easy and naïve. The gap between me and the opposite sex showing itself through this immaturity of my mind which caused by the way my parents warning me about men. When you are 26 years old and you are still single, it means that you are afraid of something. Yeah, I'm afraid of falling for a wrong man again and I am afraid of misunderstanding of kindness as love. This fear has been my nightmare about 10 years. And I blame Restricted land for this. The creation of so many stupid boundaries which results in our sadness, our madness, our isolation is Restricted land's fault. I don't want to be so close to a guy because I think I can't control my feelings. Maybe I could. I don't know. I have never been in a serious relationship. It's better to say that I have never been in a rclationship.

Note 8
On the Feelings

Here in Restricted land, a mutual relationship is only defined in one acceptable framework, marriage. I mean, no boyfriend/girlfriend relationship is allowed. So, without knowing your partner, you're going to marry someone and then, six months later, you want to get a divorce because you thought he is the one in your fantasy but in reality, he is not your soulmate. Relationship before marriage is forbidden here. I'm not talking about sex. If you want to go out with your fiancée, you must ask your parents first. I mean what kind of law is that? I think I could be an independent girl when I turned 18. I'm 26 years old and still I have to ask my parents about everything. Can I go out with my friend? Can I buy this t-shirt. I'm not kidding. This is what this is. And you are still curious to know why people emigrate! My sister is 13 years old. I don't let my parents repeat their mistake in giving her lessons of life. She has a crush on a boy and that's totally normal in my opinion. I talked to her about it and I told her this is a normal feeling and it will be gone. This was something which happened to me before and I thought it was love but it wasn't. I understand her so I don't want to blame her. I asked my parents to go easy on her. She cries, she listens to sad music but that's fine. This is what I told her. It is a phase. Everybody will experience it. So, I'll try to be there for my sister whenever she needs a shoulder to cry on. I don't treat her the way Restricted land wants me to. I don't want her to suppress her feelings. She has the right to feel the way she wants. Blaming her for her feelings will not change anything but will worsen the situation. I told her to believe in herself. She is a strong girl who is able to do anything.

About three years ago, we went to the park with our cousins. They had a plan to play football with some strangers. The strangers told my sister that she could not play football because she is a girl. 'Don't listen to them. Sex doesn't matter. And no one has the right to tell you what you have to do because you are the only decision-maker of your life. Once you let them treat you like this, you will never be able to develop your character,' I told her. She is going to be a strong girl in the future because I don't let my parents impose their own beliefs on her. You can respect your parents but think otherwise. They are your parents but it doesn't mean they are always right. I think this is it. The end of this note I mean. Both pen and paper give me this chance to reveal the dark secret of Restricted land. I don't know what is going to happen when I publish this book. Perhaps I would be in another country because I'm aware of the consequences of publishing my notes. I told you before. I don't care about myself. I care about my family. And I don't want to be the cause of their death. That's right. Writing against Restricted land will end in death or maybe I have to spend the rest of my life in jail. I don't know.

Note 9
On the Ignorance of People

Who wants to stand against his country? Nobody. But when you realise the government doesn't pay attention to the needs of the citizens, you have to remind the government about his responsibilities towards its people.

The issue in Restricted land is that the presidential candidates promise to eradicate all the obstacles but as soon as they become a member of government, they will forget their promises. And we are that stupid since we've been participating in destroying our lives by voting for almost 45 years. The candidates think they are auditioning for a role and therefore they make an effort to convince people that they are here for them in order to be their saviours. They give us beautiful speeches, talking about their future plans for making Restricted land great but funny enough, those promises will never come true. They deceive us by taking advantage of our naivety. And the Oscar goes to all those candidates who were the master of acting and making us believe in them. The common point between all of them is that they are good talkers but when it comes to fulfilling their duties, all of a sudden, they become somebody else. Inflation ruins our lives but the Leader & Co. become richer. I shouldn't expect a lot. I live in a third-world country. People are ignorant. Yes, they are. I realised it when I heard on the news that many booksellers are about to close their bookstore and instead of them we will have new cafes. People in here are not familiar with reading. Eating is much more important. We live in a third-world country because all we have learned from western culture is how to dye our hair, how to put a lipstick on our lips and... So, you may confront with a beautiful face which is empty from inside. Restricted land is the repetition of huge mistake of the Americans in the Jazz Age. They made a mistake about 100 years ago and now we want to imitate them after all these years. We are paying attention to appearances so we have nothing to say. Personally, I think it's not that bad. We're entertaining ourselves with appearances so we will stay in the state of ignorance. When you are an ignorant person, you don't care what's happening around you. When you believe in the words of your national TV, then you are not going to be able to distinguish reality from fiction. And that is what Restricted land wants.

Those who emigrate from here, were the men of thoughts. They do not believe in what their society tries to impose on them as the reality of the world. They are using their eyes to observe. They are reading books to be educated. They are analysing the situation to understand the reality. And then they decide about their life. They are the winners. People are blind in Restricted land. You turn on the TV and you're going to see that the reporter gives information about the war in Palestine, the segregation of black and white in America, the egotism of president of France, but when it comes to Restricted land, the reporter said over 4 million people are fully vaccinated. This is how the system makes you believe in diplomacy of this regime and its government. Showing the good points of Restricted land and covering the bad news of other countries at the same time depicts the corruption of Restricted land. The present system wants to make us believe that we may have some problems but they are not as important and serious as what other countries are dealing with. There is no war and segregation here. What else do you want people?

Note 10
On the Totalitarian Regime

Let me answer the question about what else do we want as human beings. We may sleep tight at night without hearing the sound of an explosion, but we should work all day to earn about 100$ in a month.

We're not familiar with segregation between white and black, but we definitely know what patriarchal society is. I'm familiar with the law of Restricted land. It is not written for the sake of women. Women in this society are condemned to be subordinate to men.

Women can't sing because their voice can provoke men. Women can't get married marry without their father's permission and if they do, their marriage will be illegal. Women can't travel abroad without their fathers or husbands' permission. You may think I'm exaggerating but I'm telling the truth. Thc system wants to bold the bright side of Restricted land. That's totally normal. But I wish the system has the courage to talk about the dark side of this community and the unexplainable boundaries which originates in dogmatism of a narrow-minded person. This regime is a totalitarian regime as I mentioned before. This regime is capable of doing every kind of violence for its survival and therefore this kind of system can't be a friend but our enemy. This is a fact. You hide something from somebody means you are a criminal. You consider women as marginalised group means you are stuck with stupid traditions and beliefs. Yes, that's what you're to me Restricted land. *Oedipus*, the king, brought plague with him in Thebes. He was the source of predicament of Theban. Because of his corruption. Just one person could change the lives of million people. He believed that he is a righteous man but he was wrong. At the end of the play, he understands he is the one who brought corruption to his city. He had the guts to admit it. But the problem in Restricted land is that the Leader & Co. are unable to admit they are wrong. This is dangerous. One single leader has an impact upon his society. You might have heard about ISIS. They killed innocent people because they believe in what their leader told them to. And if in Restricted land we can't see any progress, it is because our leader is against the progress and development. Education is dangerous and well-educated people would jeopardise the system's function.

So, people should stay in the state of unawareness in order to not revolt against the regime. The irrational boundaries are now should be considered as the laws of this society and those who want to break these rules are rioters. It doesn't matter if the laws do not serve people's progress, as long as it covers the leader's will, it is viable. Our leader wants us to be oblivious, so we should be oblivious. Those who are aware of conditions are the enemy of this system so they have to be killed. If the leader of ISIS believes in killing innocent people, the members of ISIS will imitate what their leader does without questioning it. If the leader of Restricted land is a traditional man with dogmatic opinions, the rest of the society will be as traditional and dogmatic as the leader. Those who revolt against these wrong traditions, they will be accused of being a traitor. So, they have to die because they are toxic in the eyes of the system. They will help other people to open their eyes and to see the reality. Therefore, you either die with honour or live with shame. Another resolution is to escape from Restricted land and find happiness somewhere else.

Note 11
On Inflation

I can't just stop talking about inflation because it is an important issue in Restricted land. Our salary isn't enough to have a normal life. Who can live with 100$ in a month? It is not enough. You have to pay the bills, taxes, you have to buy food. 1kg meat is about 35$. There are many people who earn less than 100$ and you think they are really able to eat meat? Nope. There was a video on Instagram which made me upset. There was a man who said that he hasn't eaten meat for three or four years. And still the system insists on portraying the war in other countries rather than spending his time on his own faults. People in Restricted land are dying because of hunger and our national TV aims to depict the political issues in other countries. People need food. Their income isn't enough so they will become criminals. How is that possible that a 13-year-old boy killed an 8-year-old girl for money! Why the streets of different cities in Restricted land are replete with innocent girls who fuck men for money? Do they want to be a whore? Or the society makes them whore? Companies are looking for their ideal workers. You know what an ideal worker is? Someone who work for hours with a little amount of salary. They were born to be a worker. They were born to help their masters become richer and richer. I live in a country which thinks women should not wear tight clothes because men will be provoked. But selling themselves to men is not counted as a kind of corruption at all. What would you do if you were them? They are rejected by their society, there is no job for them, the Leader & Co. do not even have enough time to waste on such trivial issues. They only concentrate on what is happening around the world which is none of our business. You blame other countries for indiscrimination and segregation, then, why don't you blame yourself for being this indifferent towards your people? How many gummy worms a girl can suck in a day for earning money? Is that what she loves to do? Is that the virtue you were talking about? Then why she cries in her isolation? Who makes her a porn star? Having an abortion for several times represents your virtue? Maybe your dictionary is different from what I have. Have you ever dedicated your time to listen to these girls? Nobody was born a whore here, but they become a whore due to the lack of job.

If your concern is to bring salvation in the lives of people, you will have to listen to them. A thief wasn't born a thief, his wretchedness makes him a thief. Have you ever seen a girl, standing across the street, all dolled up, but for whom? For a stranger! Is she going to experience the real love in her life? Or her destiny is to spend her life in the street, waiting for a sick guy to pick her up and be her saviour. Yes, he is her saviour. Then, you want to prove that life isn't unfair in Restricted land. She could have her own family and a happy ending story than having sex with different guys for money. But in Restricted land people's story is such a tragedy. And people are getting used to this tragic end in here. To be honest some people can't tolerate this amount of bitterness in their lives and they finish their misery by a sweet suicide. As a reminder, I have to tell you that I saw that guy who committed self-immolation because he lost everything he had. Why don't you have the balls to talk about these people. They live here. You promised to take care of your people, providing their happiness and peace. Is that what you want? Maybe I'm stupid and I don't understand anything about your policy, but I know what humanity is? I think you are unfamiliar with this word. Every single person who dies in here will shout "what a joy" like *Ivan* in *The Death of Ivan Ilych* because they finally find happiness. Something that you were unable to bring in Restricted land. Their restricted souls now are free souls. Here, to live is to die and to die is to live. Here, everything is different from other parts of the world. This note was more painful than what I expected. Reality makes me sad. I wish I could be indifferent about everything but I can't.

Note 12
On My Sister's Birthday

Today is a special day. It's my little sister's birthday. Because of Corona virus we're going to have a small party. She hasn't had fun for almost 2 years. I mean, generally we're not having so much fun in Restricted land. But we used to go to a park with our relatives at least. She is 13 years old now. She asked me if it is possible to invite her beloved! I just smiled. 'You know the rules honey, that's not possible,' I told her. She is the one who wants to go studying abroad. I am supportive of her decision because I'm sure she is going to have more space to discover. She is not born to stay in Restricted land. She is too young to be confined by the system. Okay, I'm 26 but she is 13. She can be a noble woman. Anyway, if she moves to the other country, I will be the happiest person in the world since she can be the person she wants to be. Not a person my parents or the system want her to be. The issue is that we're not that rich. We have a normal life. I mean we can eat meat and pay the pills but the problem is that studying abroad at her age would cost a lot. Sometimes people wish for something but they could not achieve what they want only because of their situation. I'm not justifying. I'm telling the truth. If we sell everything, we can support her for only 2 years or 3 years.

It's a fact. When I was 18, I wanted to go abroad but now I'm 26 and I'm still stuck with this country. But finally, I made my decision. Although I passed PhD exam and I was invited for the interview, I didn't go. I can't get along with this system anymore. As soon as I get my PhD, I should stay at home because there would be no job for me. In Restricted land, you should be either a doctor or a defalcator. These two are well-paid occupations.

You have no idea how many boys and girls give up on their abilities and dreams because of earning money. A girl can be a great painter but if she wants to guarantee her future life, she has to be a doctor. An English literature professor only earn 300$ within a month. It's sad but true. No wonder why everyone seeks to escape from Restricted land. There is no guarantee for their future. With this amount of money, they would never be able to have a family with beautiful kids. Those who don't earn enough money they must forget about having a baby. They even have to forget about marriage let alone having a baby. Living together means you both can manage a life financially but only 10% of people are able to fulfil their dreams and the other 90% should cope with the economic plight. Do you remember when I mentioned inflation as the source of our predicament? I wasn't lying. Only 10% of people in Restricted land are living whereas the other 90% are trying to pretend that they are living. The thing is that corruption is derived from poverty and when people find themselves in a situation in which they are no longer able to be a noble person, they will do anything to survive. At this point, Restricted land is a chaotic society. Inflation and poverty make people do things which is opposite to the definition of humanity. Living in Restricted land can be seen as living in the wilderness. We think we have rules but there is no rule in here. The only rule is to keep people in unawareness so they will never realise what this regime does to them. If a girl becomes a whore, the system would rationalise it as her problem. Because she has no roots, she will do anything. That's her choice, it's her fault not the system's. But my question is that is she really want to be a whore? Does she prefer to fuck guys for money over a peaceful life with his man?

Are we idiots? The answer is that we live in a society with lack of employments opportunities. There is no well-paid job except 2 or 3. This day was supposed to be a good day since it's my little sister's birthday but now I'm worried about her future. I don't want her to sell her soul. I want her to be a person who I'm proud of the most. I don't want her to worry about her future. I want her to be as happy as possible. I don't want to see her getting used to poverty and ignorance like the majority of Restricted landian people did. That's what I wish for. Please, don't let the system treat you like an animal little sis. You are not a puppet. You are not a toy. But you are a strong girl who can change her fate by escaping from here. Don't waste your moments in the only-10%-of-people-are-able-to-live country. Don't give permission to patriarchal society to suppress your feeling. Always remember that. You have to promise me that you will be a woman who will stand against the dogmatic creed of this system. You are 13 years old now little sis. Happy birthday! Don't let them tell you who you are. You are a great and beautiful girl. I appreciate your honesty. I'm in love with your kindness. You are a perfect girl. You are different from those who only think about their looks. This is a community which is replete with masks and lies. And I'm so proud of you because you are not corrupted.

Note 13
On Subordination

Do you remember when I chose a pen name for myself? I think Offred is not a fictional character anymore because we, Restricted landian women, are the incarnation of Offred. Our totalitarian regime degrades women as much as possible. Polygamy is allowed in this country. Only men can have more than one wife at the same time. I don't mean to bring this subject to tell you why women can't have more than one husband. But my concern is that why my society encourages man to have five wives at the same time. What's the point of it? Showing off men's power over women! Or maybe because we live in a patriarchal society and men are allowed to do what they want. You know that wearing perfume is forbidden for women according to the law, right? Again, because the scent of women would provoke men. God, I really want to laugh at this third-world way of thinking. You want to justify women are subordinate to men, but what I see is that you degrade your men until they will be seen as an animal who is not capable of controlling himself. You just dedicate power to men because they have penis? That was what Sigmund Freud used to think of men. You have penis, you have power. Are we still using this kind of abrogated theory in Restricted land?

The answer would be yes. My society can't just accept woman as an independent entity by herself. It doesn't want to give her permission to be as free as men so the result would be nothing but justifying our female imprisonment as the protection of men and society from corruption. I know it seems nonsense but I'm telling you the truth. Men in Restricted land are the representative of *Tom Buchanan* in *The Great Gatsby.* They are a bunch of narrow-minded guys who tries to introduce themselves as a tactful person. They are as shallow as *Tom*. There was a part in *Gatsby* which made me laugh out loud and it was when Tom gives a speech about black and white people and he quotes from a book to portray himself as a well-educated man but he doesn't even know the correct name of the book, let alone its content.

See, he is a shallow man. We all know that he saw women as his commodity. His perspective is as the same as Restricted landian men's point of view towards women. Now imagine a society in which all of his men are Tom and all of the women are Offred. Is there any chance of progress in this society? In a society in which his men are all seeing themselves at the top of their given hierarchy, is there any chance for women to be free and independent in every aspect? There would be no chance, not in the slightest. Restricted land is a corrupted country and nothing will be changed until people gain a proper insight about living. The Leader & Co. would not let us breathe, as long as our breath belongs to somebody else. We are a slave. That is what we really are.

Note 14
On Womanhood

Well, after one of our female weight lifters won the world championship, some people in Restricted land blaming her because of her chosen field in sport. They didn't encourage her for what she did. There was an interview with one of the well-known actors about this woman and what he said was that women's job is something else. 'She has to stay at home and be a perfect mother but weight lifting would ruin her womanhood since she chose to do something which we consider as a manly sport,' he said. After that, there were a wave of comments about her, showing the agreement of people with this actor. Before that, I always thought that an actor has to be a role model for others so he has to think before he speaks but now, I understand that even some of our actors are the stooges of this regime.

'I'm not misogynist, you can ask my wife. But women should know their role in the society,' the actor said. From this interview and all the comments, you will understand that women's role is defined by our patriarchal society and even if we stand against it, like what our champion did, the people of Restricted land will blame these women. I'm not against motherhood. But I totally disagree with this statement that a woman should be either a mother or a selfish woman who prefer to do what she likes. Women can do anything. Motherhood is beautiful but maybe some women do not want to be a mother. This is their choice. Maybe a woman wants to be single. But this actor's general statement about women is an imposing push which forces women to accept their role as a person whose only job is to carry a baby. So, women in Restricted land are surrounded by the given culture with its origin in the people's ignorance and the system's skills in misguiding us. From the beginning of my notes until now, I put my emphasis on people's ignorance and I have my own reasons. People never question, if the system does its job correctly or not. The malfunction of the system is hidden because of their ignorance not because they are blind. There were many societies with totalitarian regimes around the world whose people had the guts to criticise the malfunction of the governments and the system. But when it comes to us, we do as we're told like we're a slave. I totally agree with rules. A society without rules would be a wilderness. But what kind of rules? The rules which bring peace and quality, progress and salvation. But the rules of Restricted land are derived from suppression of people's feelings and thoughts combined with social and political constraints. That is what I call freedom from constraint. Every society would be afraid of rising of its people so the government will do anything to suffocate the voice of freedom.

In Restricted land, the Leader & Co. know that if people rebel, then everything will change and because of that, they have to be careful about what's happening around them if they want to continue with their ruling status. I think it was 2019 when people's lives in Restricted land were occupied with inflation and then the price of gas was doubled, out of the blue. The sudden changes brought unhappiness into our lives and 90% of people in Restricted land were mad at their government.

They rebelled against the government, and they stood firm against the irrationality of the Leader & Co. So, people started texting each other in order to be united. But the rising of people against their government for having a normal life was in vain. The government realised if people rebelled against the system, life of the totalitarian regime would be in danger. Firstly, the disconnection of the internet happened and we didn't have the accessibility to the internet for one week. Then, the armed guard killed many innocent people and put them into prison. Well, their crime was that they wanted their normal life back. But to be honest, they have to be thankful. I mean people. You know why? Well, those who are in prison now, they do not know anything about inflation and they live happily ever after and those who were killed by the armed guard, are free now. Thank you, government for helping them pursuing peace and happiness! It was not the first time you made us happy. You remember about Flight no. 666? Oh, you don't. Okay. As far as I remember, you killed another group of innocent people intentionally. No, no, sorry. Unintentionally, yes. You killed 176 people, unintentionally. What was I thinking? For a second, I think of you as a killer.

Accept my apology by the way. I didn't mean it. Accusing you for an unintentional accident was unprofessional. I mean there were only 176 people, right? Who cares? This kind of accident could happen everywhere. I mean we have to be thankful it's not an annual event. It was just one time. And we all forget about it. I'm sorry, if I mentioned that. But did you were sorry for this unintentional accident? Oh, no. You weren't. And what was your justification for this accident? If I'm not mistaken, the Leader & Co. just gave a speech, asking people to forget about it because it was an "accident". Personally, if I kill an ant accidentally, I will be much more upset than you. They were not everybody, most of them were from Restricted land who find their happiness in other countries and hats off to you for killing all those intelligent people. I know what your problem is. You have issues with being an intelligent. You want a country full of stupid people so you can rule as you wish. Tell me if I'm wrong! Who am I talking to? A bunch of carless rulers? Come on… I almost forget you were deaf when it comes to criticising the malfunctions of the government. You are only responsible for what you did intentionally. So that accident is none of your business since you did not know you were going to kill innocent people. You owe their families an apology. A big one. I'm not asking you for being sorry for what you did because I know it's too much for you, but what I'm asking for is an apology. At least, pretend that you are sorry. I'm aware of your ability to act. Restricted land is a stage for you and you act perfectly. So, just act please or lie to our faces, like you always did. I thought, it would be a piece of cake for you to act and lie like a professional actor. What happened Leader? You have been lying to us more than 40 years.

You have been acting like you are our saviour all these years, then why don't you just lie that you are sorry for what happened. Why don't you listen to the poor parents, wives, and husbands who lost their beloved? At least you could pretend you're listening. At least, you could pretend you care about them. And by them, I mean your people not a bunch of foreigners, your people. Your people who were born in Restricted land and you were responsible for them as a leader. Why you don't care about us Leader? Is there any distraction in your way? We want to live Leader. It's all I want. Why you give us such a hard time? Why everything in our country is different from other countries? Being a dictator doesn't mean that you are a perfect Leader but you are a coward person whose concern is to lose his social status. Why are you killing innocent people? Why are you letting criminals live? Is there any chance for the next generation to live as a normal person? Let us live. I beg you. Let us live. We are not your enemy. We are your people. Don't accuse other countries for our retrogression. Accuse yourself for what you have done all these years. If we are unfamiliar with development is because you have an issue with progress. The intelligent people escaped only because you don't let them grow. It's all your fault Mr. Leader. Restricted land was supposed to be God's country. The country of noble people. Don't you think something is wrong with our country? I mean God's country is Restricted land now. How on earth did this happen? Somebody needs an explanation here.

Mr Orwell in *1984* states that 'nothing was your own except the few cubic centimetres in your skull.' But Mr Orwell, in Restricted land, we are not the owner of our skulls either. Your imaginary community was much better than this society. I mean, at least people of your fictional work are the owner of their skulls. But our skulls are occupied with the given culture. We think otherwise, we will definitely die. If you were alive Mr Orwell, you would write another *1984* or *Animal Farm* about Restricted land. I think this note is much longer than I expected. I need some sleep. My mind is tired but my fingers want to write. Mr. Leader, I hope you will read this note carefully one day. And just pretend you are sorry for what you have done. I don't want you to kill yourself, pretending is enough.

Note 15
On Freedom

As far as I know, in many countries people are free to choose their partner. I have never been abroad but at least I'm aware of things. I know about Pride month. I know about LGBTQ. So, I know people can choose their partner. It's up to them who they want to go out with. I mean, there would be some obstacles for people who choose to be gay or lesbian in other countries but those problems are not as noticeable as what we're dealing with in Restricted land. Let me tell you about the tragic destiny of a boy in Restricted land who chose to be gay. He was gay but he was not allowed to be gay in Restricted land. In this country, the only acceptable relationship is men and women getting married. That's it. So, you have to be careful who you are falling in love with. And more importantly, sexual intercourse is not allowed before marriage. This is what this is. You can't change the law. You don't want to be known as a whore in your country with a scarlet letter on your chest, do you? Okay, where was I?

Yeah, the boy who was gay. Well, he was beheaded by his brothers by the way. The end. I told you before, we live in a jungle. And in a jungle, animals are allowed to do anything. I just saw his picture. He was too young to be killed. He was supposed to move to Europe to live with his partner. For your information, that romantic day turned to a tragic night. A tragic end for a boy who was born in Restricted land. He made a huge mistake. He knew the system. He knew the rules. But he chose to be a freeman. He chose to spend his life with a person he loves. And he was punished for this. He is another Offred. with a little difference that he was notforced to be with another person but he was killed by his brother. Wasn't blood thicker than water? Instead of being supportive of your brother, you killed him. Hats off to you, my friend. You killed your brother because you think he was a sinner. But killing your brother isn't supposed to be a sin? What if he chose to be a sinner? His sin was to love a guy. And yours was to kill your brother. Which one is unforgivable? Who the hell you think you are? God? Making decision for somebody else's life is stupid. Yes, in Restricted land, our personal life and our relationship with another person is up to everybody. There is no privacy. There is no respect for what we choose. Our society can't stand this disrespect to its established rules and laws. Once you break them, you are a criminal. Before, I decided to write this book, I thought writing would help me to purge my soul from the madness I'm suffering from. But I gotta tell you that I am not happy right now. I'm still mad at this totalitarian regime. I have to leave this country as soon as possible because I don't want to be a madwoman. Asylum is not an option for me. Come on… I'm only 26 not 90.

I still have time to live the way I want. At least, I'm happy because I'm not lesbian. Who knows what would happen, if I was attracted to women! I know my parents love me. There is no hesitation. But I don't know what would be their reaction if I wasn't the person who I am now. They sacrificed themselves to nurture me and my sister. But sometimes we fight over trivial things only because of diversity of opinions. For instance, they are not comfortable with the way I behave. I'm friendly and I don't care if my friend is a boy or a girl but my parents' issue is that they want me to be as cold as possible when I talk to the opposite sex, including my friend. I know, it seems ridiculous but it is true. I swear to God that I am not exaggerating. I'm not writing a fictional work but the reality. It's like a documentary, recording what I observed in Restricted land. I mean the guy who was beheaded by his brother is not a fictional character. The story of that specific flight with 176 passengers wasn't a lie either. I know, I live in Restricted land and I shouldn't be trusted but I'm not lying. I'm not a leader. I'm just a person. Trust me, it is not a fictional work with fictional characters. It is based on reality. Just google it. Then you will realise that I'm telling you the truth. Don't tell me that the name of my country is fake. We live in Restricted land. If I find an opportunity to publish this book, then I will give a lecture about it with visual images and videos. That's all I can do to show you I'm not a liar. Nobody likes to stand against her country. I don't want that either. I am not sick to write about something which does not exist. I don't want to waste my time to write a nightmare. If my country was a perfect community to live in, I would portray a utopian society instead of a hell. But Restricted land is a dystopia. Then don't blame me for being rude to my country and the government.

When you have been deprived of the simplest rights in your country, then you can't just sit and let the government play with you like a barbie doll. Nobody has the right to give us instructions about whom we have to fall in love with or what piece of garments we are not supposed to wear. We are not living in North Korea. Now, it's the time for us, Restricted landian people, to sing along *Read All About It* by Emeli Sande:

You've got the words to
change a nation but you're
biting your tongue
You've spent a lifetime stuck
in silence afraid you'll say
something wrong
If no one ever hears it
how we gonna learn your song?
So come on, come on
Come on, come on
You've got a heart as loud as lions,
so why let your voice be tamed?
Maybe we're a little different,
there's no need to be ashamed
You've got the light to fight
the shadows so stop hiding it away
Come on, come on
I wanna sing, I wanna shout
I wanna scream 'til the words dry out
So put it in all of the papers
I'm not afraid
They can read all about it,
read all about it,
Oh, ohhh, oh
Ohhh, ohhh, oh
Ohhh, oh, oh

At night we're waking up the neighbors
while we sing away the blues
Making sure that we're
remembered, yeah, 'cause we
all matter too
If the truth has been forbidden,
then we're breaking all the rules
So come on, come on
Come on, come on
Let's get the TV and the radio
to play our tune again
It's 'bout time we got some
airplay of our version of events
There's no need to be afraid,
I will sing with you, my friend
Come on, come on
I wanna sing, I wanna shout
I wanna scream 'til the words dry out
So put it in all of the papers
I'm not afraid
They can read all about it,
read all about it, oh
Yeah, we're all wonderful,
wonderful people
So when did we all get so fearful?
Now we're finally finding our voices
So take a chance, come help me sing this
Yeah, we're all wonderful,
wonderful people
So when did we all get so fearful?
Now we're finally finding our voices

So take a chance, come help me sing this
I wanna sing, I wanna shout
I wanna scream 'til the words dry out
So put it in all of the papers,
I'm not afraid
They can read all about it
Read all about it
Oh, ohhh, oh
Ohhh, ohhh, oh
Ohhh, oh, oh
I wanna sing, I wanna shout
I wanna scream 'til the words dry out
So put it in all of the papers,
I'm not afraid
They can read all about it,
Read all about it,
Oh, ohhh, oh
Ohhh, ohhh, oh
Ohhh, oh, oh

Note 16
Farewell

I just can't stop listening to Emeli Sande's song. I think this song is written for Restricted land. We have to be together, if we want to change this corrupted nation. Maybe it's time. What are we waiting for? We are our saviour. There would be no magic or miracle. Only we, people can change the current situation. Don't pray. We need to act. We may lose. But at least we can tell our kids that we tried.

'You publish your book you will be executed by the regime,' My mother told me the other day. 'If you publish your book abroad, then there would be no coming back. You can't come back to your hometown, to your family, to us,' she warned me. I'm all aware of the consequences, Mum. Publishing this book means a huge farewell to the past. Not only to the past but to the most important people of my life. So, I want to dedicate this note to you. To my dad who was my hero although we used to fight over things but he is my dad. I love you, Dad. I'll miss your paternal concerns. Mum! You are great. You have a sharp tongue but you are the kindest mother I have ever seen. Little sis, I don't know what should I say. I want you to stay strong. Be kind to people. Don't fill your heart with hatred but love. I love you. I love all of you. Thanks for everything. You were good to me. I did my best to be a perfect daughter for you but if I wasn't, forgive me. I want to make you proud, if I'll become your biggest regret, please accept my apology for not being a person you are proud of. I want to go and I want to escape becauseI don't want to be a troublemaker. I won't jeopardise your lives. You will be safe in my heart. We are different. Maybe you are too optimistic about what is going on in our lives but all these years I've been trying to be realistic. We've been too busy to talk about stuff. But our love is inevitable. It wasn't supposed to be a Shakespearean adieu. I don't even know why I'm crying. I asked my little sister to be strong and now I am crying like a baby. So, I think this is it. It was the hardest thing I've ever done. I'm not good at acting. I just told you what I feel. The only thing I want to see is your hap…

Note 17
On the TV Programs

After writing the previous note, I thought I can't continue writing but here I am. Last night, I cried. I don't know why but I couldn't help it. I was lost in my thoughts. About the future and the past. About the present. My sister cried too. We all are worried about the future by the way. 'Are you going to be able to come back for my wedding?' My sister asked. I smiled. I couldn't lie to her. I'm not a soothsayer. I have no idea what will happen in the future. I mean, we both want to go abroad since we couldn't find what we need in Restricted land. 'You may find your love abroad, and then I'll be there for you. For your wedding,' I said. Our destination is different. She likes Spain. I love somewhere else. From the very beginning of my childhood, I was in love with directing and cinema. I'm going to tell people my favourite stories without worrying about censorship. I'll tell the story of those Restricted landian people who are no longer alive to tell their own stories. The story of a guy who was in love with another man, the story of a girl who was forced to get married to a 70-year-old man because of money, the story of a Restricted landian girl whose society makes her to be a whore, and the story of a 26-year-old girl who wants to be free. TV programs in Restricted land are nonsense. The gist of TV shows is that living in a poor family is not that bad and poor people are the happiest people in Restricted land but living in a rich family means people are greedy and there is no happiness in the lives of the rich people. You may ask what is wrong with these kinds of TV shows. Everything seems natural. But if you think carefully, you'll understand what the problem is. These TV shows want to make us believe that there is no problem with people who don't have money, people who are hungry, or people who are dealing with so many issues in your life.

As long as they are alive, they have to be thankful. The general portrayal of rich families in our national TV is shown by depicting depressed greedy shallow unhappy people. Almost in all of the TV shows, the good guy is a poor one and the bad guy is a rich one. It is a tricky ideology that our society wants to impose it upon us. Living in poverty with innumerable problems shouldn't be counted as a negative point since being rich means being a bad person. But I can't get that why our politicians and the leaders of the society are incapable of giving up on their belongings. They look happy to me. They have everything they want. Mansions, great cars, fancy vacations, delicious food, and more importantly they have no problem. This contrast must be something. I mean, if being poor is the total happiness why the poor people aren't happy? And if being rich means isolation and depression, then why in reality they are jubilant? Maybe, I misunderstand this ideology. Let me interpret it the way the system wants me to. The breadwinner of a poor family is ashamed of his unemployment since he can't buy foods and stuff. And the mother of the family is the housewife, her job is to take care of her children, that's all. So, we have a housewife and an unemployed man from the working class of the society. But funny enough they all are happy together with no reason. They are hungry but that's okay. They are happy instead. They wear each other's clothes since they are poor. But that's fine again because they are happy. I mean, you only have to be crazy to be happy in this situation. And that is how the majority of people in Restricted land think, that happiness is not derived from money. This is what the society is teaching them.

I don't want to say that money is everything but at least I know it is not just nothing. If money doesn't bring comfort, then why the leaders of my society are in love with stealing money from people? It is not comprehensible. Maybe they lost their way. We have to guide them to walk on the ground of misery and plight than comfort and opulence. This is for you then:

Dear Leader & Co. please be careful about what you are doing now. Money is nothing. I'm here to warn you. Leave your mansions as soon as possible, throw your money into the river, burn your cars, and please stop travelling. I can see the symptoms of unhappiness in your lives. Money is nothing. Please, join us. Be hungry. Be poor. Be miserable. It's not fair. We are laughing and you are upset. Let us make you laugh again. Your luxurious life turns you to a madman. You are not able to distinguish between good and evil. Let us help you. You were our leaders but you lost the way. Happiness is in rubbish bin where the poor people are looking for a piece of dried bread. Why are you looking for happiness in stuffed lamb? I mean there are enough rubbish bins out there. We don't need to fight over them. We can search for food and whatever we need in them. Purge your soul from unhappiness and depression by being our comrades in this way. We want you to taste the real happiness. Once you taste the real happiness, you will realise what we have been going through. I didn't mean to be rude. I didn't want to give you an instruction either. I just want to help you experiencing what we have been experiencing as a true happiness all these years.

Best wishes, Offred.

Note 18
On the 18th Birthday

Note number 18! Well, 18 is an important number in every country, right? I mean, an 18-year-old boy or girl will be considered as a mature person who is eligible to vote and more importantly do some stuff which he or she was not allowed to do before. But in my country, there is no difference between an 8-year-old person and an 18-year-old person. Was I clear? Wasn't I? I mean we can vote but we can't have a partner. We can't make our own decision either and we can't live by ourselves. Especially, girls. But at least we can fantasise how it would be like, if we were free. When somebody turns 18 in Restricted land, it means he or she is one year older now. That's all. Parents do not let their children to feel what independency is. They are babysitting their children while in many countries an 18-year-old person can stand on his own feet. Our parents threaten us with generalising some rare stories which happened before to some girls. You must remember the note in which I opened my heart, telling you that I wasn't able to trust men only because my parents portrayed them as a monster. I used to think all men are bad except my father. Having boyfriends means you are begging for love from a stranger and this is a huge mistake. So, I have never had a boyfriend. Many girls in Restricted land will definitely understand what I am saying because they were the victims of some Restricted landian beliefs. To be honest, right now there are many girls and boys who are in relationships with their opposite sex and their parents do not know about it. Nobody has the right to define our needs. I don't know why our parents think that they are always right when they aren't. It is like kids are a flock of sheep and our parents are shepherds, watching us like there is always a wolf whose job is to take us away. They describe our society as a place replete with wolves. And they warn us if we leave our safety zone, which is the realm of our shepherds, then we will be sorry for the rest of our lives. An injury which is caused by a wolf would be counted as our scarlet letter. For those who are confusing now, I am talking about the excuses which our parents use in order to make us believe that we always need another person to guide us. At this point, we will always remain a person whose existence depends on his shepherd's existence and that would be a shame. Why? Because we can't think by ourselves. We are incapable of making decisions even when we become older. My cousin is a 30-year-old boy whose parents set a bunch of stupid boundaries for him. He must be home before sunset. He doesn't work because he is the only child and my uncle gives him money. He should not be alone at home because something bad could happen to him. And this big guy could never live by himself since his parents have been babysitting him for 30 years. Me and my sister need our parent's permission and opinion almost for everything. If we want to hang out with our friends, my parents should know exactly where we are going, what we are going to do there and when we will be home. This much concern is so mean.

Sometimes I think they don't trust us and it hurts me. Why they interrogate us like we are suspects. We are not going to kill somebody. We are just some friends who wants to have fun together. That's it. I gotta tell you that. When I moved to the other city to study, my parents were unable to accept it. They wanted me to go to the dormitory but I refused to go there. Dormitory in Restricted land is like a hell or a prison. So, what they did was that they found an apartment for me which was worse than dormitory. My neighbour was an old couple who was appointed to reports everything about me. If I turned off the lights for a couple of hours in the evenings, they came upstairs to be sure they did their job perfectly and the suspect wouldn't go anywhere. Oh, my God. It was like hell. I don't know, I have to laugh at this or I have to cry. But I'm dead serious. I don't need to exaggerate to tell my story. One of my friends came visiting me. You have no idea what happened that night. The old woman came upstairs and asked me to call my mum. I didn't know why. But when she asked me to pass the phone to her, I understood she just wanted to do her job. 'There is a girl in your daughter's apartment, did your daughter tell you about her?' The old woman said. I could not tolerate this much disrespect but what could I do? She was 84 years old. So, I let her do what she wants. My friend was shocked by her behaviour. It was not just that. I had many issues there. There were like my parents. They let themselves treat me like a criminal. Okay. Maybe it was my fault too. But they were too old to argue with. So, I let them have their own fun. Their door was always open to check me out. One day she came upstairs and told me about her grandchildren. 'I have a grandchild whose father didn't give him permission to go to the other city to study and he forced her to get married. I don't understand why your parents let you live all by yourself,' she said. I had no idea what she was talking about. I thought she was joking about her grandchild. But she wasn't. She proudly told me the story of ruining her grandchild's future by his father. Well, I realise it now, some shepherds need to be guided by other shepherds.

Note 19
On the Relationship

We, girls, have to struggle with many issues in our country. Let me tell you the story behind our hymen. We can't have sex before getting married. It's illegal in our country. But some girls love having sex. These girls may ruin their future by having sexual intercourse. In Restricted land, girls have to check their virginity before getting married. The guy who proposed, wants to know that if his future wife is virgin or not. If she is a virgin, their marriage will be still on, but if she is not a virgin, she will be punished by her family. That girl could never get married only because she did something wrong. I don't know if we could name an inevitable need for sex an evil deed, but I know that it's only up to her what she did in the past. I mean if a guy had sex, there would be no problem because he is a man. But the situation is different when a girl has sex before the legal celebration of her marriage. I remember, I talked about inflation. You may want to ask why did I bring this subject again! Inflation has the strong connection with marriage. When you are not able to support your own life financially, you will be afraid of commitment and marriage. This is what the most of Restricted landian boys confirmed. Then they just use girls to satisfy themselves and whenever they feel that they cannot get along with them, they throw the poor girls away like a piece of trash. These poor girls are known as a whore in my country then. And no one is willing to marry them since they are not virgin anymore. But our parents tell us that if a boy used to have sexual relationships in his live, it would be his concern, but if a girl used to involve in such relationships, it would be society's concern.

So, we are marginalised group. We are forced to accept the stupid rules of Restricted land and if we don't, we will be humiliated by our own society. Can I just lament about this? If I am not mistaken, my virginity should have been my concern. It's up to me that what am I going to do with my life. But unfortunately, my hymen is important to 85 million people.

My cousin's friend is 20 years old now. She got pregnant when she was 18. Her boyfriend told him if she got rid of the baby, he would marry her. Well, to cut the story short, she had an abortion, and the boy disappeared. I don't know whose fault is this. The girl who trusted this boy, the boy who is afraid of commitment, or my society which is the director of such dramas. The problem is that my society thinks by confining people and setting of irrational boundaries and limitation, we will find salvation. But is that salvation? I don't think so. Can I just tell other people about some stupid beliefs that you pour into society? You turn the TV on, you will confront with some spokeswoman and spokesman who teach the lessons of life. 'Be aware of that, you will have no right to yell at your husband even if he does yell at you. Pay attention to how you behave. If your husband doesn't give you permission to do what you want, you have to forget about it because this is God's will,' the spokeswoman said. I can't understand how this stupid woman let herself be such a narrow-minded woman. What a load of crap! This is what I think about every word of her speech. When the national TV is occupied by a bunch of uneducated people, then why am I expecting too much from them? Maybe because I don't expect a woman asked other woman to be an object to their husbands in this modern world. This way of thinking would suit sixteenth or seventeenth centuries. Maybe we are way past seeking for freedom and progress.

We all get used to nonsense without bothering ourselves to react against these old doctrines. Whatever it is, I just want to thank my society for paying attention to our hymen. I really appreciate your concerns about women. I know, we, women are too weak to take care of ourselves and too stupid to understand our benefits. So, on behalf of every Restricted landian woman, may I thank my society for being this careful about us! God bless Restricted land! Shame on me and all those women who think our society objectifies us. Women! We are all ungrateful. Because in Restricted land our husbands can yell at us! Name one of those countries in which a man can yell at his wife and then his wife be thankful for his violence? You will find nowhere. So, we have to be proud that we are living in a special country. By thinking about it, you'll understand that our society is based on BDSM. You have to enjoy it women. We are slave and our job is to please our master. Let's be honest. It is not that bad. We let men take advantage of our stupidity. What's the big deal? I mean, we should not expect our society understands the value of women since we are living in a third-world patriarchal society. Everything in here is based on the given hierarchy, in which men are always at the top and women are condemned to be at the bottom. We are object. They are subject. So, what is the job of an object? Correct. Our job is to keep our silence and let the subject do whatever he wants to us since we are subordinate to them. It makes me feel that we are an *Isabella* from *Wuthering Heights*. Our inside *Catherine* was killed by the society from the beginning of our childhood and we all are an *Isabella* now, a perfect object which grabs the attention of many subjects to itself. We let *Heathcliff* of our lives treat us like a dog. Bid farewell to your soul women which is captured my men. Bid farewell to your mind which is taken by your patriarchal society.

Note 20
On the Restricted Landian Parents

When I was a student at school, my parents used to compare me with other students or my cousin whose GPA was always great. They were incapable of understanding me. I hated math and biology but for them that was unacceptable because they wanted me to become a doctor or an engineer in the future. 'Look at your cousin. She can be your role model. She is perfect in everything. She is going to be a doctor in the future but if you want to continue like this, then you will be her secretary or her waitress. Do you want that?' my parents said. I was a kid. I didn't like it when they compared me with another person. I was good at literature and history but these courses were not as important as math and biology in my parents' eyes. I used to write poem but they didn't were supportive of me. I used to write play but they didn't even bother themselves to ask me about its content. Everything was summarised in math and biology and other courses were useless. My cousin is a doctor now. They were right. And I am a useless person. I am not jealous of her. I am so happy for my cousin. But my problem is that I could never be able to forget what my parents did to me. They treat my sister the way they used to treat me. Okay, I know that I'm not going to make money like a doctor, but at least I know I choose to do something which I like. I would never be a successful doctor. I wish they could understand that their interference would destroy our future.

I have another cousin who has been wasting three years of her life to become a doctor only because of her parents. I know this is mean. But what can we do about it? I find a solution. I do not listen to them anymore. Like I am a deaf person. I can't change them because they have been thinking like this for 55 years. They get used to this way of thinking so changing their opinion wouldnot be as easy as you think. It is almost impossible. So,I let them say whatever they want. And I'll do whatever I think is right based on my own perspective. I do not let them be my shepherds at this point. Every time they humiliate my sister, I remember the past and how they ruined my pride by humiliating me. One day I'll become one of the most successful writers and directors in the world, and I will retrieve my stolen pride fromthem. I will show them that I am not a pathetic loser. To be honest, I did not have a normal childhood either. I was not allowed to watch dance. I was not allowed to listen to music which made me dance. As far as I remember, they gave me a ball and asked me to play with it. I did not know how to be a girl. The past is gone. The present is my torture. I hope my future will be my dreamy life. I want to fulfil my dreams, those which have been ignored for 26 years. Thosedreams which have been denied because I wanted to fulfil my parents' dreams. I wasn't successful in achieving their goals. But I lost my chances to be the exact person of my imagination.

I only daydreamed about what it is like to be my imaginary girl. I still have time. My sister too. We both can flee from Restricted land, settling in one of the greatest free lands in the world to be who we want to be. Experiencing a normal and a peaceful life is all I need. A place where nobody is blaming you for who you are. A place where no one is allowed to give you instruction like you are an animal in a circus. A place where your sexuality is up to you and no one can give himself permission to impose his doctrines upon you. I've never been abroad but I have no doubt that I can find such places to live. Not all societies in the world are the killer of souls and minds. There is no perfect nation. But there is a society in which people feel happiness at least. I can't talk about other nations since I have a little information about them. But I have this permission to talk about my own nation. No one wants to live here. People are tired of living in Restricted land. I am tired of living in a dogmatic country. It is like our voice are muted. I want to live somewhere that my voice will be heard. My society is too busy to listen to my issues. I have to asked another society to listen to me. We are a poor generation. Neither our parents nor our society understand us. And here we are! All of us have so much in common. We are a broken generation. Our society didn't take pity on us. It was like a professional killer whose job was to purge our souls from liveliness. We are a depressed, nervous and dead nation. The 200-year-old doctrines was the murderer of 85 million people's spirits. There is no life, when there is no energy and spirit. We get used to it. We get used to it. We get u… I did not mean to make fun of our society but this is what this is. We might lie to other nations about how happy we are but we can't lie to ourselves, can we? I did not mean to let you down either but the reality is that we are a dead nation. I know we breathe but we are dead.

Note 21
On Mass Media

I have just finished watching a series. I wasted my time to be honest. I talked about TV programs and TV shows before but I want to introduce the other category to you. There is another type of movies and series which are produced and written by the so-called broad-minded directors and producers. What they are portraying in their shows is nothing but how easily men are cheating on their wives, and how classy a professional smoker is. In these kinds of series, all the characters are from high class of the society and the plot is not a triangular love but a pentagonal love. A married man is falling in love with a married woman and the man has another girlfriend and so on. The director of such TV shows calls himself a realistic director but I strongly believe that he is in love with fantasy. Why? Because his man-made society is devoid of other strata. All the characters come from high class of the society. Do we have such a society? I don't think so. Women are the commodity and they have to be played by men. Although female characters are educated, but they are naïve and weak in their confrontation with men. Getting a divorce is something natural in these series and men can throw their wives away whenever they want. This well-known director produced many series and movies with the same content. He naturalises betrayal and divorce. The bad person is the attractive one who could be a great role model for the society. There is no law as age-based restriction. So, a 9-year-old boy or girl can easily watch these series and since they are not mature enough, they will be attracted to the bad guy of the story and trying to imitate him as a role model. That is why some school girls and boys are a professional smoker nowadays in Restricted land. After the school, they are gathering together to talks about their role model while they are smoking.

Those who watch such shows accept that having an affair is something natural in people's live, women were born to be the puppet of men. Smoking pot or cigarette is fun. This director doesn't think about how he could affect his society by producing such things. But he doesn't even care about it. Maybe he is not conscious of the contents of his movies and series. But I think a director should be the voice of his people. I mean a realist director. When about 90% of people in his society are the middle class or the working class, he should not put his effort on producing same contents with different actors and actress. He has been into creating just trash contents for seven years. Can I just compare his masterpieces with *Friends*? I know they are two different genres. But *Friends* is the representation of routine of normal people. People who care about each other. They watch each other's back, betrayal is unforgiven, falling in love with best friend's ex-girlfriend is not normal. This is the major difference between a director who pretends he is a realist director and the one who seeks to teach lessons of life. If having an affair is not acceptable in *Friends*, in both TV shows and movies of the unnamed Restricted landian director cheating is normal. Our leaders are corrupted, the national TV is corrupted as well. When people go to theatre, they will confront with a movie which its content is nothing but portrayal of negativity. Here is my question then: when Restricted landian people are going to learn about humanity? Since mass media is the realm of uneducated and dogmatic people, is there any chance to learn good deeds? You can't just say that I am surrounded by evils but I will remain an innocent person.

Those evils have an impact upon you willy-nilly. We all have the capacity to be a sinner. So, now imagine a society in which every particle is corrupted and there is no clue of humanity, do you think that you are capable of being a good person and protect you honour from evaporation? Who do you think you are? Jesus? Of course, we can't. When a director naturalises betrayal in his series, then people accept it as inevitable part of their lives and they try not to react against it. I gotta tell you that almost every man in Restricted land cheated on his wife at least one time. This is not a guess. This is what I see. For a married man, having an affair becomes an entertainment. And you know what the poor wives do? They accept it. For the sake of their honour, their pride, and their kids, they try not to argue with their husbands about this issue. So, men are allowed to cheat on their wives whenever they want and women give their consent to this huge and unforgivable vice. The normalisation of being a pervert is another issue which women have to struggle with in their lives. They prefer to ignore their husband's corruption since they don't want to be known as a divorcee. There is no wrong with being a divorcee in other countries but as you know Restricted land is something else! In here if you get a divorce, people will look at you as a faithless woman. They all think that it is your fault since you were unable to protect your family thus you have to be alone for the rest of your life. Nobody is going to take your side when you want to get a divorce. Everyone would think that there is something wrong with you as a wife and as a mother. The man was the one who crossed the line but unfortunately you are the one who will be seen as a guilty person.

But there are many women in my country who are dealing with their husbands' betrayal because of the irrational point of view of the society about being a divorcee. This is another philosophy which is written by the narrow-minded philosophers in Restricted land. Everything is originated in the patriarchal ideologies and therefore women have no place in this society. Everything is against them and they have to admit it. If a woman has an affair, she will be punished in the most barbarian way. Have you ever heard of lapidation or stoning? You might not know about it since you are not living in a third-world country. It is a kind of punishment which is established as the penalty for a married woman who slept with another man. She will be tied up and people start throwing stone at her until she dies. The other two penalties are hanging and whipping. If there was any equality in this country, then all the above punishments should use for a man who cheated on his wife. But because this society is not a big fan of women so their punishment must be more painful than men. A man can continue living like nothing happened but a woman should bear an animalistic torture. And you are still wondering why am I writing against my country. You can call me a traitor but I don't give a damn about it. Because I don't want to be a commodity. Is that really hard to be understood? Well, I thought I was talking about movies and series. We have feminist director as well. But I am sure she doesn't know anything about feminism. One of her movies was about a couple who were unable to get along with each other and they think divorce is the only solution. According to this director, a feminist character needs to portray a woman who can humiliate his husband in front of other people or forcing her son to apologise in front of every person because of something he didn't even do. The director wants to embody a powerful woman who is able to violate the patriarchal viewpoints but this is not what we consider as feminism. What she did is to make people become so pessimistic towards what feminism is. I'm talking about the real feminism not those irrational thought of some thinkers who believe that the world would be a better place without men. There should be a balance, if we are looking for a moderate society. But this feminist director only grabs people attention by representation of a dogmatic woman as a feminist. If in those shows of that male director women were the commodity, in the movies of this female director women are filled with hatred towards men. The common point is that the women are not lovable anymore. She wanted to create a character who is independent and strong in her life, but she messed up. This irrational mother-in-law is not a strong woman but a monster. And you will not find a man who is in love with a monster. I wish our directors stop producing such nonsense. People watch and learn. You can't just say it was a movie. That's all. They have to be aware of the content they are producing. They want to sell their movies and because of that they think, they can tell every story which pops to their minds. Open your eyes, please. You are responsible for what you create. Don't give us trash. We, as the viewer of your movies and series want you to not take advantage of your status. If you call yourself a realist director, then please don't mess up the content. Don't you realise that you are capable of changing people's point of views towards different aspects of life? Don't you understand your movies have the power of settling itself into the minds of people? If you can't do your job, then just leave it to the professionals, those who can realise what is the predicament of modern people in Restricted land. You don't need to waste your time only because you want to make money. Do something less dangerous. Providing a general framework for people is not an easy job. See. You messed up.

Creation of a movie is easy. But the content is important. At least watch some masterpieces to learn what a great movie should have. Do you know what comedy is? It is not making people laugh by telling jokes. Because you are not a clown. You have to use comedy to talk about people's issue. Personal or social, it doesn't matter. But our comedy is shallow. It doesn't have any content. Okay, I admit that M.M. is the only director who use his dark comedy to portray people's issues. His comedy depicts the gap between the proletariat and the bourgeoisie. His series represent the corruption of Restricted land. He knows his people. You know what bothers me a lot? I know that I am waiting for Godot but I won't admit it. I would like to change people but I can't. Why am I expecting too much from a society in which I am the only one who can hear me! It seems that people are pretty happy with their lives, I mean, if they weren't, they would let the society hear their voice at least. Maybe I am in the wrong place. My mother loves here. My father loves here. My sister is somewhere in between. I am the only one who has a problem with my hometown. So, I think I have to adjust myself with the situation. All I need is to become as indifferent as possible, then nothing would bother me. It works for other people. It would definitely work for me. At least, I could give it a shot.

Note 22
On the Presidential Election

If I am not mistaken, we are so close to the important event of presidential election. Of course, I am eligible to vote but I am not going to vote. I don't even hesitate. Not in the slightest. I am tired of listening to the candidates because they are bluffing. For more than 40 years, we have been deceived by them. How foolish we are! It makes me puke to listen to a bunch of repetitive lies. The candidates make fun of each other rather than talking about their plans. They could not even answer the simplest question so, how possibly they can become a president of a nation? What makes them think that they are worthy to be chosen as the second important person of Restricted land. All I can see is a bunch of stupid people, gathering together to amuse people by their jokes. It seems that they have no plan for the future of Restricted land and the only reason for their nomination is to accuse each other for the present issues of this community. For them, being a president is like a game rather than a serious job. Instead of talking about their plans they disrespect each other. In my opinion, they are not capable of becoming a president. I've learned a lot from previous contestation that the candidates know how to sweet-talk us into voting for them. As soon as they win the election, they forget about their promises. Without a doubt, I can tell you that they are suffering from Alzheimer's disease. I do not know how much money a president is going tomake but it must be noticeable amount of money since the candidates give their best shot to deceive people. I don't care about the parties. Conservative or Reformist, they are all liars to me. They talk about poverty or people's unhappiness but they don't do anything about it. I can talk too. There was a rural man who came toregister for Presidential election, when they asked him why he is here and what makes him think that he can rule a country, his answer was telling. 'I am here to make people laugh, isn't what the other candidates do? Social justice means to put everything in its right place. I am not eligible for being a president. I just register for fun,' he told the interviewer. I was shocked by his answer. What he means was that all the candidates are nothing but a clown whose job is to entertain us by joking around. They have no idea about the responsibilities of a president, they are only tired of staying at home so the first solution which comes to their mind is to register for the presidential election. And I am sorry for Council of Guardians whose job is to disqualify the unqualified candidates. They accept those who the Supreme Leader wants them to. And then we are wondering why the society is corrupted. The right people are in the wrong place and the wrong people are taking the control of a nation. The root of our unhappiness is originated in the inaptitude of Leader whose ideology leads to the predicament of the modern people. Instead of accusing himself, he accused foreign countries. Instead of letting the right person sit in the right place, he asks Council of Guardians to announce their disqualification. I don't understand the notion of presidential election in Restricted land. The motto of our Leader is honesty but he is incapable of being honest. For the sake of his totalitarian regime, he does everything. He says he cares about people but he doesn't. If he does, he will never let himself be an obstacle to the progress of his country. It is all about being selfish. It is all about the infinite greed for power. For the stability of his given system, he needs to fill his government with his wolves. An owl would jeopardise his dictatorship. He will kill all the owls who knows his dark secrets. One of the greatest poets, Fereydoon Moshiri wrote a poem, *The Wolf*, many years ago but I just realise how this poem suits the present situation of Restricted land. This poem is translated by Faranak Moshiri in English.

A tenacious wolf, said a wise man once,
Is hidden deep within each of us.
Hence, an immense daily struggle is ongoing,
Between the wolf and the human being.
Might alone will not this wolf subdue,
One with intellect would know what to do.
Many a man, weak and grieved,
Have their wolves by the throat seized.
And, many a man, courageous and strong,
Have been trapped in their wolves' claws for long.
Whoever defeats his wolf, gradually,
Becomes a wholesome man, eventually.
And, one who's always defeated by his wolf,
May appear to be a human, but he's a wolf!
And, one with whose wolf he will conspire,
Wolf-like nature he will acquire.
When you're young, your wolf's life you must take,

To let him grow old with you is a grave mistake.
Even a lion of a man when he's old,
Is no match for a wolf who's grown old.
Whenever people tear each other apart,
Wolves are their guide and steward.
Why humans are in so much pain?
Because it's their wolves who have the reign.
And, tyrants who keep one another in confidence,
Their wolves are each other's acquaintance.
Alliance of the wolves, estrangement of the men,
Of this strange state, to whom may one complain?

Note 23
On the Blind Imitation and Social Media

I only referred to the blind imitation of people in Restricted land without expanding on this issue. Let's talk about it. By the birth and the development of social media, people become closer to each other than the past and the accessibility to share our life and thoughts with other people give us the opportunity to make friends and become familiar with different people from other cultures. This connection which was established by social media, have had an undeniable impact upon our lives. Every development has its own advantages and disadvantages so, we can't consider a progress in technology as a total win. Therefore, social media can be observed as a cause of jeopardising lives of uneducated people who doesn't know how to use it and at this point, every development has some victims. Those illiterate nations will have the most victims. Restricted land as a third-world country is in danger of collapse since people do not know how to use social media in their daily lives. Since they are a newcomer to social media, they seek to find a famous role model for themselves to learn how they can gain a reputation for being a blogger or whatever they want to name it. This would be the beginning of the blind imitation of a person. This issue can be a serious one when about 80% of Restricted landian users only install such application to become famous. They are not using social media as a platform for becoming familiar with various cultures and traditions but for 80% of people, social media is the place for publicly parading themselves. The other point is that these people do everything to grab the attentions of others. Talking about the most personal issues of their life, and sharing it with other people would be an inappropriate action.

In Restricted land, even a 9-year-old boy has access to social media and he can search things which he is curious about. One of the viral lives on a social platform was about a woman who asked an 11-year-old boy to talk about his sexual life. The boy started his conversation by claiming that he always masturbates by watching the videos and pictures of that lady. And almost 2 or 3 million people in Restricted land watched that live. Every application is age-restricted but in my country, parents doesn't care about this issue. An 8-year-old boy has access to different applications even the destructive ones. Almost every child has its own phone or tablet. Even a 3-year-old kid. Instead of going out and playing, they stay at home and wasting their precious time by playing with their phone. Parents think that being a supervisor means forcing their kids to act and behave as they are told or to limit the circle of their friendship. But social media for them is harmless since they are keeping their kids at home. They have no idea what kind of danger is waiting for their kids only by using a small phone. That 11-year-old boy ruined his life because he was not supposed to use the application, which one of its requirements is to be at least 17 years old. I don't want to accuse him. He is a kid he is curious about stuff but I want to accuse his parents for letting him install the application which is unnecessary for a boy at his age. I want to accuse that woman who encourages the boy to tell her about his masturbation. There would be many girls and boys who watched this live and now they want to know what jerking off means. Kids are curious about new things and they would go and search for it to learn about inappropriate subjects. The easy accessibility to different social applications will lead to the corruption of kids. Kids need to experience what being a kid means rather than ruining their childhood by using their phones 24/7.

In Restricted land, kids are unfamiliar with books and novels. The presence of social media in their lives makes them an inane person whose life is summarised in sleeping, eating, and using mobile phone. They do not even bother themselves to watch a documentary or an informative movie. They are busy killing enemies in their phones or scrolling up and down the screen to find the newest challenges becoming trend on social media. You go to their rooms, you will not find them reading books or playing with their toys, but you will definitely catch them playing with their phone. When these kids become older, their attitudes will change. They are all become an edgy person with the least capability of being in their society due to the fact that they have spent most of their life plying with their phones. Like my little sis. My parents bought her an expensive phone only because all of her classmate had phones and she hadn't. I told them not to buy her a phone but they did not listen to me. Well, the result is that she gains weight by sleeping and playingwith her phone day and night. She barely comes out of her room because she is busy with her phone, playing games non-stop. I did not let her install social media applications. My parents admit that buying a phone was a huge mistake but she is addicted to her phone and personally, I think we can't do anything about it. Some mistakes in our lives are irrecoverable. She is always up all night and sleeps in the morning instead. Sometimes she fell asleep during her online class. It is not only about my sister. It's about the majority of kids in Restricted land whose parents kills their childhood by buying mobile phones. At least, they have to set some limitations such as how many hours they can use their phone, or what kind of application they can install, but they don't do anything. Most of the parents think that their responsibility is only to buy a mobile phone for their kids. So, what that kid is going to do with his phone is his concern not his parents. The other problem is that 80% of users of social media forget their real identity in order to be a perfect person in the eyes of their followers. And who are the followers? Some people who look at that specific person as their God and as their role model. So, they will be the reflection of what they are looking at. And as I told you since people in Restricted land think using social media is the only option to grab people's attention, the content is not important. When the great proportion of social media is occupied by the illiterate people, the content of their posts, videos, or lives would be absurd but attractive. I have to put my emphasis on this point that by the great proportion I meant 80%, the other 20% are counted as the true users of social media. If someone posts the picture of her luxurious birthday, all of her follower will learn this trick by posting same pictures and contents to steal people's attention. So, tomorrow, when you are opening your social media, you are going to confront with so many clichés. If she posts a picture of herself shaving her legs in the bathroom, tomorrow the bold subject of social media will be the anatomy of shaved legs of women. To be honest, you have to admit that this issue does not only belong to Restricted land, other countries are dealing with this issue as well. Restricted land is an example. And because I live in this country, I can talk about its problem. Other countries are not my concern. Let's move on. I want to interpret social media as a company. What is the function of a company? I think we all know that. Companies are producers. Social media is a producer as well. If companies produce goods, social media produces human's attitudes and lifestyle.

You may ask yourself how many cosmetic companies have been established in recent years! and you may want to know how many publishers have struggled with the issue of bankruptcy! I think you understand what my point is. Okay, let me be more specific. After the development of social media, people's lives underwent a big change. They sacrifice themselves for the social media to be as similar as possible to the majority of people. If the demands for cosmetic is three times as high as the demands for books, it is only because the social media company creates a framework for its users that grabs their attention to appearances. For instance, a woman used to believe that she is more beautiful without makeup but now she is comparing herself with a famous influencer or a blogger. She finds herself a person who needs to change her look to compete with these successful women. Social media is the competition platform now. It means that people are competing with one another to win the golden medal for being the most pretentious human being in the whole world. Therefore, for achieving such a valuable goal they have to show off with their belongings. By a simple search, you can find such accounts which are replete with various posts of the account owner's cars, her expensive dress, the picture of her nails, and many more pictures from what she has. But if you asked her to name three female novelists, she will die. Do you remember when I criticised movies and series inRestricted land and I felt sorry for the directors of such movies who were out of the content? Now I feel sorry for those who are teaching people how life can be restricted to appearance. I think the American dream is too far from us. We are not going to achieve this dream when in the clashes of appearances and humanity, appearance is the constant winner. I am not against beauty and I don't want to be a dogmatic person. I am not saying that life means reading books, thinking about higher education and… My problem is that the seductive propaganda misguides people. Beauty does not limit to our looks. Beauty is practicing of being kind and honest. Beauty means helping people who are dying from hunger. There is no need to buy the most expensive stuff for your baby who doesn't even understand what Fendi or Gucci are. Posting the picture of your babies with their fancy dress is not beautiful. It is lame. You are teaching people the wrong lessons of lives. Is that your understanding of beauty? You are maybe filthy rich but from inside you are an empty person. There is no moderation in your lives. You don't even take a pity on your own kids when you are using them as part of your competition with each other. From the very beginning of their childhood, you gave them everything and they are going to look at you as their personal bank, so they would not bother themselves to try for what they need. Your kids will be the products of your behaviour. I am talking to my parents right now. If you bought my sister whatever she wanted, then you should not expect her to stand on her feet in the near future. She will be dependent on your money because you put this idea in her mind that she can have everything if she cries. And who will be a loser in the future? She will be the loser without a doubt. She will always go for a small dream which does not require hardworking and patience because she will find it hard. Do not raise your kids like this. I, myself, know that by hardworking I can achieve my dreams. It may take my time but it worth the effort. I want to know how independency feels like! I have to thank my parents for growing me like this. If they bought me whatever I want, I would not be a hardworking person then. Like what I am now. I hope parents realise what they did to their own kids one day.

At least, I hope the next generation find their way. And finally, I hope the toxic atmosphere of social media will supersede by healthy one. I read somewhere that the problem of Restricted land is not the anonymity of the wise men but the lionisation of the foolish men. I couldn't agree more.

Note 24
On the School Punishments

I remember when I was a student, my school was my nightmare. I was afraid of punishment in front of my classmate. We all were afraid of this horrible situation. Even if our principal punishes one of our classmates in front of us, we all were sad. It was a real bummer. I mean we had to swallow our pride and honour when somebody had a plan to degrade us. In this country from the beginning of our life till the end, we all have been punished by our parents, the schools, the universities, and the society. Observing my friends when they were questioned and beaten for a bad grade was my nightmare. We were 10 or 11 years old when we were experiencing the notion of school punishments. Well, here is the confession. One day me and one of my friends did not do our homework. I thought there would be no problem but when our teacher asked us to give her our homework, I realised I messed up. I was petrified with fear. All of my classmates did their homework. But I was lucky because I wasn't the only student who hadn't done her homework. My friend, N, she didn't do her homework either. We were the only 2 out of God knows how many students we were, who did not do their duties correctly. When our teacher noticed that, she called for the principal immediately. It was the first time we didn't do our homework and we didn't expect that much bestiality. At least, she could give us some advice or whatever. But her solution for punishing these nonchalant students was calling for the principal. It was so sweet of her. We begged. We cried. We asked her not to call the principal. But, sadly enough, it didn't work. She was a *Cruella*. We begged someone who didn't know what forgiveness was. Maybe she wanted to threaten the other students by punishing us so they would not come to the class without their homework done. 'At least, it was better than calling our parents,' I whispered. Because that would be another level of punishment. We realised we couldn't stop her from calling for the principal, so, we stopped begging. There was only crying then. The principal came.

The teacher revealed the secrets of her nonchalant students. I was standing in the corner. The principal only beat N. She lost her balance and she fell down on the floor but the principal didn't stop beating her. She was crying. For me, it was like waiting for my execution. At that time, I didn't even care about my pride, the only thing I was thinking of was punishment. After 2 minutes of beating N, the principal left. N was laying on the floor and I was confused. I was happy too. I can't lie. Not that happy. I was only happy because I wasn't beaten to death by the mean principal. I helped N to stand on her feet. She was shaking. She wasn't able to speak. She was shocked, so was I. 'So, our parents are not the only people who have permission to beat us, to punish us,' I whispered to myself. I didn't have the guts to talk because I was afraid of *Cruella*. I didn't want to be punished by the principal. Personally, I had no idea why she skipped punishing me but whatever it was, I was both sorry and happy. If I didn't stand in the corner, I wouldn't be this lucky. I was happy because I was only humiliated by the teacher. It was not comparable with the torture that my friend experienced.

After all these years, I find myself a guilty person because I was coward to be punished alongside my friend. Like a kitten I hid myself. I didn't want to feel the principal's hard fists. But poor N, she was terrified like a little girl who lost her parents in the crowd. I think it was too soon to become familiar with the concept of punishment at school. I mean, we were only 10. Of course, I disagree with any kinds of punishments like what we experienced. But because I am familiar with the educational systems of Restricted land now, that punishment wasn't so bad. At least, she could be more gentle for the first time. I mean, she could give us some advice. She could only warn us that she is not going to give us permission to attend the class the next session if we don't do our homework. This would work, I think. She shouldn't have wasted her time by asking the principal to punish us. I mean punish N. But you know what is funny about this story? After about 16 years, I haven't been able to forget it. I used to define teacher as a friend or as a person who can teach me valuable lessons of life. I thought a teacher is the symbol of patience and kindness. But after that day even if I want to think positively, I can't. I didn't tell my parents about it because I was afraid of being humiliated by my parents too. I could not bear this much humiliation in one day. I was a kid and that foolish teacher was incapable of understanding this. It was one of the worst childhood memories I've ever had in my life. Well, I can keep going, telling you about how does educational system define itself in Restricted land. It is like a never-ending story. And definitely I can tell you about my personal experiences during all those years when I used to be a student in Restricted land.

Well, I was a middle school student. I was 14 years old. It was the last day of school for us. Since it was the last day we could see each other, we had a plan to have some fun together. We were taken to a restaurant by the school bus driver because we wanted to buy sandwiches and having fun in the bus while he gave us a ride home. We were not allowed to eat out so we had to eat in the bus. We all talked about this with our parents before and they agreed. The bus stopped in front of the restaurant and we made a decision that it would make more sense if only two of us got off the bus, ordering food for all of us. The distance between the bus and the restaurant was only 20 steps. It was a pavement so the bus couldn't be any closer. We bought sandwiches and we enjoyed every minute of our little girlish happiness in the bus. One by one we got off the bus. When I went home, my father was standing there, waiting for me maybe an hour. He was so mad. 'What took you so long,' he asked. 'I told you yesterday about our plan. We just bought sandwiches, eating them while we were on our way home. Why are you asking that?' I asked. 'Don't lie. One of your teachers saw you and your friend while you were walking in the street. Where were you?' he asked angrily. 'Why should I lie. There is no reason to lie. Me and my friend just got off the bus to buy sandwiches. That's all. I have no idea about what that liar teacher said. I am telling you the truth,' I said. He didn't believe me. He reprimanded me for being a liar. Because he trusted a random teacher from nowhere than his daughter. I could not persuade him that my teacher made a mistake. He was standing on his words that I am a liar. I stopped defending myself. I let him purge himself from anger.

What was I supposed to do when he didn't even listen! He was insisting on the point that I am a liar. But I wasn't. Whenever I think about it; I find myself unable to forgive that stupid teacher and my father. But I am not a revengeful person so I forgive them for what they did to me. I called my friend who was with me asking about her mother and her reaction. I wanted to know if she told her off since his father passed away many years ago. I found out she was so lucky because her mother believed her. Nobody in my home believed me. The worst thing is that when you are telling the truth and nobody believes your words. You know what will come to your mind then! That you will be punished finally either you tell the truth or you lie. Then why am I bothering myself to be an honest person with my family if they will punish me though. When there is no difference between lying and telling the truth, why shouldn't I lie? But I am not a liar. I don't lie to my parents. My father didn't even look at my innocent face when I was crying non-stop. I hated being questioned like a culprit for a crime which I didn't even commit. I was punished by my father because of the stupidity of one of my teachers and the naivety of my father since he believed every single word of a liar. I don't know how would I react if I were him. But I am sure about it that I won't judge my kids by another people's nonsense. At least, I let them talk and then I would judge who is the liar and who isn't. But my father judged me without even listening to my confession. That is not fair. I was sentenced to be known as a liar who shouldn't have been trusted. Then I started blaming myself. Right now, I think if that day I wasn't volunteer for buying foods for other students, I would not be punished. This is only a hypothesis. And let's not talk about something which hasn't been proven yet. Well, if you think my sweet memories of school are summarised in these two cases, I have to tell you that you're wrong. My memories about school are infinite. There is no end.

I might have heard about other students in other schools and how their teachers and principals punish them. But let me only talk about my personal experiences which are based on fact. No exaggeration. No hypothesis. Only fact. In middle school, I have many memories but I want to tell you about my memories from high school. I told you before, I wasn't good at math or physics or everything which is related to math and numbers. We had physics exam and I got 2. The worst grade in the class. Many of the students got 20. The teacher gave my paper to the principal. It was like that my own teacher was dumb herself, and she couldn't talk to me about the exam. That's why she asked for the help. She asked the principal to talk to me. The principal in my high school was an illiterate woman. She did not beat me and she didn't call my parents either but what she did was kind of rude. 'Look, you got 2. If I were you, I would at least got 10, although I know nothing about physics,' she said. First, I have to thank her because she talked to me in private. Second, hats off to her for being this clever that she can get a good grade although she knows nothing about physics. But she humiliated me by her sharp tongue. She might have thought that; this would be the best way to advice but believe me it was shocking. To me, her words could be interpreted in this way that I was a birdbrain student who learned nothing. In my defence, I have to tell my high school principal this: you remember about all the top students of your school whom you were proud of? Well, most of them can't even finish their B.A. No offense, but it's a fact.

I know about them. I don't mean to be rude or something. You all humiliated me but would you please look at me now. I am standing where I wanted to. On the behalf of all those students who have been humiliated by their schools, I have to tell you that only a stupid educational system requires stupid principal. Again, I am talking about 80% of schools in Restricted land. I don't want to generalise my opinion. The 20% of principals and teachers are too good to be true. That is a fact. I am talking to the other 80% whose educational system is beyond what we know as the worst. And if they want to know why their educational system is not lovely, I can explain it to them. The age of punishment was about many years ago, when human beings were in the state of ignorance and they didn't use their brain. Dear teachers would you please do yourselves a favour? Don't mock yourselves by utilising the system of punishment which belongs to the age of revenge tragedy. Be creative at least a little more. The next generation of students are going to be so lucky to experience new forms of punishments. I am so jealous of these students. You lucky bastards! I have a recommendation for teachers and principals, if you want to punish your students, you have to watch *Whiplash*. It's a great movie and if you are insisting on punishing your students, this movie will give you some ideas. Go for it.

Note 25
On Suicide

Committing suicide in Restricted land has different reasons. I categorise the causes of this social issue in my society into three main sections. The first cause and the most common cause of committing suicide is poverty. There were many people who could not tolerate poverty anymore. These people were used to live like a normal person one day but different economic issues forced them to kill themselves.

The indifference of those who are responsible for bringing economic crises to the lives of people is the reason that the majority of people realise that their government is as useless as the third nipple of a guy. When the economic policy of Restricted land is under the control of someone who is only thinking about the profit of himself and his friends, then people become poorer and poorer while the Leader & Co. become richer and richer. And no rich leader can understand social and financial issues of poor people. The situation of the majority of the middle class is as the same as the working-class people. They do not earn enough money and the government doesn't pay attention to them so the best way for ending their economic plight is to kill themselves. If a person burns himself, it doesn't mean that he is weak, it means that he can't tolerate hunger and poverty. He can't buy food for himself, let alone his wife and kids. He kills himself because he doesn't want to be ashamed of his poverty in front of his hungry family. I am not talking about a Greek tragedy. This is reality I am talking about. People kill themselves because they are not important for their government. Our government is busy with the embezzlement of its members. So, I don't think that our government has enough time to think about our issues. By only thinking about the word suicide, my body shakes. I believe that if a person wants to kill himself because of poverty, he comes to this point that living is going to be more painful than dying. He knows what he is doing, he knows there is no coming back. So, when a person decides to kill himself, he definitely finds his peace in it. Someday if I'll become that poor, I may kill myself too. Nobody has the right to judge a person who killed himself because of poverty. People could never know what kind of crises that person had been going through.

In Restricted land, you will find the most useless government in the world. The members of the government only think about their own pockets so if people's pocket is empty, there will be no problem as long as their own pockets are stuffed with money. This is so tragic, seeing people have no other choice but to end their lives because of unbearable tensions. He was born in a wrong country. Maybe if he was born in the society whose government finds itself responsible for its people, he would have a better life. It is so sad to see people killing themselves that easily because of the economic policy of the government. When only 10% of people in Restricted land are rich, it means something is wrong. When 5% out of that 10% are working for the government, it means hardworking doesn't make money, dishonesty does. There was a TV program in which talented people competing with one another. The host asked one of them what would he do if he won 25000$. He said he haven't thought about it yet and when the host told him it is impossible, the boy said 'I don't think about things that I don't have.' The majority of people in Restricted land aren't even able to daydream. The reality for them is like a dark cell in prison, confining them harshly to their doomed destinies so they can't even imagine what the other possibilities are. Their minds can't process unfamiliar concepts. There is no "what if" in their lives. I feel sorry for them but the sad thing is that I can't do anything for them except writing about their stories. I mean, I helped people but that is not enough. The government is the one who should take care of its citizens. Maybe the government likes seeing people killing themselves. I can't find another reason for the indifference of the Leader. Since he is in love with killing innocent people, he may have so much fun seeing poor people evaporating. Well, people have different perspectives about a specific issue. Poverty makes me upset but it could be the reason of the Leader's happiness. I should not expect the Leader to react against people's suicide when we are living in two different worlds. This is who I am. And he is who he is. Okay, let me introduce you to the second reason of suicide in Restricted land. It is all about patriarchal society of Restricted land. There is a city which is known as the capital of women's self-immolation. This city is famous for the violence against women. Since this city is one of the greatest patriarchal cities in Restricted land, women are the victims of dogmatism of their fathers and husbands. Well, they have to respect women but they don't. Forcing them to get married to a random guy, beating them to death, treating them like their slaves, and many more reasons could be seen as the causes of women's preference of death over life. They can't escape. They only can kill themselves to get rid of the cruelty of men. And as far as Restricted land is a patriarchal society, people do not protest against the violence against women. The government wouldn't bother itself to pass an act about women's rights. The government doesn't set a penalty for violence against women. Everything is written for men since the law is written by men because they only think about their own benefits. Domestication of women is what they have been looking for in all these years. They are not going to let woman be as equal as men. They won't let women be as free as men. Women's suicide for the patriarchal society of Restricted land means women are weaker than men, it confirms the power of men over women. In addition, the general portrayal of women as a docile thing is what Restricted land wants to present proudly. When I was at school, I was afraid of punishment and humiliation, now I am just thinking about all women who bear so much violence in their lives. Imagine a life in which every day you are waking up with tensions. It must be hard for you. Then your day and night would be only thinking about how you canend this life. You will complain about your conditions in your isolation. If you show your disagreement with your husbands or fathers, you will be punished. You can only talk to yourself about your sadness. Why a father should force her daughter to marry someone when there is no love between them? I think I could answer that. A narrow-minded father knows well that he would not live as long as Noah so he should look for another narrow-minded person who can watch his daughter rather than loving her. Love would be dangerous at this point. If a man loves a woman, he will let her be a free woman. He gives her love and respect. He treats her like a princess. He never tries to make her upset. But if a random guy from nowhere proposes, only because the girl's father asked him to, the poor girl should say yes without hesitation. He doesn't believe in love, so his daughter is forced to marry someone who is replete with anger and hatred. They have the right to live like a normal person but if they couldn't find this opportunity, they would kill themselves. Dying is one hundred times better than accepting such disrespect. This is the crises of a third-world country in which women should deal with men's hatred. Well, the third and the last category for committing suicide is kind of complex. It is about boys and girls who are falling in love with one another.

The story beings when their parents cannot accept that they could make a perfect couple together. Parents always criticise their offspring for their choices. They think that they know everything so they give themselves permission to interfere in the personal life of their children but forcing them to marry someone else is an unforgivable mistake. The love story of that couple would end with the tragic suicide of both of them. How easy parents play with their children's life. They prefer to see a version of *Romeo and Juliet* rather than letting their kids marry the person whom they love the most. Arguing with parents doesn't work. Believe me. If parents do not let you do something, they really mean it. Sometimes some miracles happen, but most of the time parents are the real winner in this combat. This kind of suicide is the worst one. Because they want to live, they have no financial or social problem. They are not tired of living but they have plans for their future and all of these dreams and goals are going to be ruined in one minute by their parents. So, this is it, I think. I'll try to cover the most important reasons of suicide in Restricted land. Restricted land is really a restricted land. The name suits it perfectly because of all these restrictions and limitations. If I want to be realistic, good deeds are the limitations, evil deeds are so welcome in my country. And again, my mum asked me why I am not talking about the good things. In my defence, I have to tell you that I really want to portray a utopian society and make the other nations jealous, but I am not good at lying. I have to help people open their eyes to the reality of our country. Creating phantoms of happiness is an easy job. Like what the government does. It pretends like there is no serious issue in this country. So, as a person, my responsibility is to remind them that they are wrong. I can be a bootlicker like all of the members of the government, but between a bootlicker and a traitor, I choose to be a traitor. This society is replete with bootlickers, now it is the time for some so-called traitors to revolt against the bootlickers' movement.

They are dangerous for the society and we have to wipe them out until the society becomes clean again. Then instead of the totalitarian regime we will have an appropriate system which can be trusted. A perfect system which is based on justice and it brings peace to the lives of men and women because there would be no subordination anymore. We are all equal.

Note 26
On the Addiction of the Youngsters

The most embarrassing moment for parents is that when they become aware of their kids' addiction. They are not trying to study the reasons why their kids have a tendency towards doing drugs. They do not even act like a supportive mother or father. If you are curious to know what parents will do when they realise their kids are addicted to drugs, let's get started than. Well, their one and only resolution is to force them to leave the house because of their pride. They do not want to be criticised for the addiction of their children and therefore they act like they never had a child. They forget their kids for the sake of their honour. 'What if our families and friends find out about this? Everyone is going to laugh at us because of our child's addiction to drugs. What would be the society's reaction,' parents always say. They do not ask themselves what they can do for their kids to help him or her to forget about doing drugs. They have no rehab program for the poor youngsters. Going to rehab is scary and those who are addicted to drugs need someone by their side. But when these people are ignored by their parents, they came to the conclusion that if they are rejected by their parents, then they will be rejected by the society and when nobody is there for them to go to rehab, they will become a professional drug user. A drug addict needs somebody in his side to support him but once he was rejected by everyone, he will be disappointed. He finds himself alone in the cruel battle with his addiction, thus for distracting himself, he will do drugs to both forget the past and the present and to enjoy the fleeting moment of happiness. Why a boy or a girl become a drug addict?

They are curious to know about things and they want to test everything which is new to them without knowing about its consequences since their parents have never talked about many issues. They never talk about drugs and its horrible consequences because they think by mentioning this topic, their kids will learn about different drugs and they may become a drug addict. Because of this wrong way of thinking they do not try to educate them. What will happen now? Since that boy or girl is not aware of what drugs may cause, when one of their friends ask them to join in doing drugs for feeling happy and relaxed, they can't turn it down. When that amateur boy or girl finds drugs exciting for the first time, they will do drugs like a champ. And after 4 months this person will be unable to stop doing drugs. His parents will notice some changes in his attitudes and his look such as, his unusual tiredness, his impatience, his violence against people, his pale face, and so many other clues which are the characteristic of a hop-head person but they do not think he becomes a drug addict, not even in the slightest. When the situation becomes worse and the parents finally find out about his addiction, they will punish him by throwing him away from the house. They were guilty for leaving their child alone. He is so vulnerable now and he can do something stupid. No money means no drugs and therefore he decides to earn money in different illegal ways such as mugging and stealing. He is a needy person now and his existence depends on drugs. Without doing drugs he will turn to a dangerous person who is capable of killing someone without a doubt. You feel sorry for them because of their detachment from their society. They make a house for themselves by the old clothes or cardboards in the suburb so they can live in peace. They made their own independent community since they are rejected by their society. Their parents forget about their existence let alone the society. Now heroin and LSD are their best friends. They smoke to death. They are no longer conscious of their behaviour and their action. Their brains are as empty as possible. What a horrible situation! In Restricted land although the market for illegal drugs is not allowed but near to one million people took drugs at least on time in their lives. 10% of these drug users are women. The most shocking news is that 22% of the total drug users are well-educated people. You might be a well-educated person, but when you haven't enough information about drugs, you are capable of becoming a drug user. When people do not have any background about a certain thing, they will prefer to experience it because they are not aware of its consequences. Parents, schools, universities, mass media do not pay attention to the undeniable issue of addiction. So, people will be the victims of the drug dealers whose goal is to sell their products and they do not care about their victims. This is the responsibility of the government to fight against the drug dealers. In addition, it is the duty of mass media to educate both parents and children about the consequences of doing drugs.

If an addict father beheaded his child, it's because he would hardly distinguish reality from hallucination. He thinks he is killing a kitten. Directors can produce a documentary from such drug users' life to educate people, especially the teenagers who are ignorant about what nicotine, cocaine, and other drugs can do to them. All kinds of illegal drugs are capable of destroying people's mind and body. If Restricted land has so many concerns about the rise of drugs market, then the government must allocate a budget for educating people. The healthy community is derived from healthy people and healthy people are the products of government's plan. Parents also should learn how to treat an addict person, I mean, instead of being a mean father/mother, they have to be supportive if they want their children's souls back to their bodies. By criticising them, they cannot solve the problem but they add another professional drug user to the society. The addiction of the teenagers can be seen from another perspective which is more common in Restricted land and it is nothing but receiving parents' legacy of addiction. Imagine you are living with a drug addict father, what will you learn from them? To be honest, you will learn how to snort cocaine like professionals. You will learn how to smoke dope because you have been raised in a family in which from your babyhood until now drug was the only thing you have seen. The issue is that your parents don't mind if you want to start smoking because they are drowned in snorting and smoking. Congratulations! You are a drug addict now. I know many people who embraced the legacy of their ancestors. Drug addiction and behavioural dysfunction is passed from father to son like an inevitable tradition. When they go visiting each other, they serve drugs rather than fruits or food. You may find it funny because they think that they are doing a favour to their guest and they are taking a good care of them by inviting them to smoke. That father not only ruins his life but destroys the life of his son and his future grandson or even his granddaughter. His decayed mind can't process anymore so he is not aware of what he is doing to his poor children. He thinks what he does is a favour. And let's be honest, we should not expect from a drug addict to think like a sober man. His mind does not belong to himself anymore and it is the drug who makes decision for him not himself. The most horrible things can happen when drugs controlling his mind and body. So many weird hallucinations. Drugs makes you see your wife as a wolf who is trying to kill you. What would you do in your defence? You try to defend yourself by killing the wolf who is your poor wife. There are many stories like this. Wait. It's not story. What I mentioned was reality. If the government is really fond of his people, it will be so sweet to do something in order to eradicate addiction from the society. Rehabilitation is a hard procedure and no one can do it all by himself. A drug addict should be taken care of in the first place. Then he has to understand what he did before was a huge mistake. The person should come to conclusion that smoking and taking drugs would ruin not only his life but his family's as well. Of course, Restricted land is replete with camps but most of them are illegal. They torture the addict person by imprisoning him to a dark room and forcing him to forget about his addiction to drugs. This brutal method doesn't work at all. By whiplashing him or threatening him with death, the addict person would not heal. All the illegal camps must be closed because they are managed by unprofessional men who want to earn money. The members of these camps are some unemployed people who come up with the idea of opening a camp for people who are suffering from addiction. Unfortunately, they have no knowledge in this field and they do not care about the vulnerability of a drug addict and moreover, their methods would be brutal and inappropriate. The common method of these illegal camps is to beat the addict people who is weak and cannot even defend himself and at the same time they humiliate him verbally to make him realise why he is here and why he has to be punished. As I mentioned before, the government is too busy to manage everything. The government only interfere in the issues which will jeopardise its operation. A bunch of addict people would not be a serious menace to the government so they prefer to stay out of it. I do not have knowledge about how to treat an addict person so I can't give any suggestion but when the members of the government are chosen by people as their representative, they are responsible for them. Maybe I have to remind you about your job. You are from people and for people, don't take advantages of your status by stealing people's money and not caring about them. If you are chosen by people, it means that they trusted you as their advocator whose concern is to protect his people. People are looking at you as their shelter towards different dangers. If you want to persuade me that it is not your job to educate people or to take care of your nation, then why you even exist? Why in some countries such as Finland, Norway, or Denmark people are always happy. Maybe because their governments are the representative of their citizen? Maybe because they put their people as their first priorities? Maybe because they find themselves responsible to their people? Let's be honest, what did you do to us Restricted land? Did you do anything for your people? for their happiness? Or you just abuse the power to become more powerful and rich?

There is no wonder why all Restricted landian people are about to escape from here. They seek happiness in foreign countries because our government is deaf and blind. You can call all those people who talk against Restricted land a traitor, but they are telling the truth which is so hard for you to accept. I will assure you about the fact that no one is willing to leave his hometown unless they find joy somewhere else. So, if Restricted landian people decide do emigrate, they will no longer be able to tolerate the corruption of their country. And as far as I know, this is all your fault government, because you were so careless about people who were used to trust you one day. Your real face is revealed and the mask is gone. Restricted land is either a place for you or a place for those who are striking for justice.

Note 27
On Censorship

Censorship in Restricted land plays an important role for the stability of the ideology of what the Leader & Co. established as the general framework for people. Every kind of belief which is against Restricted land and its benefits, must be censored. This is what policy means. They may not censor a certain idea but they make fun of it as if it is wrong. The policy of present system aims to ridicule the ideologies which are not acceptable in the eyes of the totalitarian regime of Restricted land. For instance, people in Restricted land are only allowed to get married with their opposite sex, women with men and men with women. Other kinds of relationships such as gay marriage is forbidden. People who are bisexual are rejected in my country and they aren't welcome at all. The intention of every movie or show about these people is to mock them. I rewatched a movie about a homosexual man the other day and I realised why the system was willing to release this movie. When I was younger, I watched this movie in the theatre. I remember that people burst into laughter while they were watching it. The movie is about a man who pretend to be a gay to get visa. The portrayal of this gay man is clownish which cracks people up. He wants to imitate a gay person so he dyes his her and changes his personality by acting like a girl. This is how a homosexual person look likes in the eyes of the system and the bootlickers of the system who let themselves produce a movie to change the public opinion about homosexuals. This is another kind of censorship which is the production of a dogmatic amalgamation between the system and the bootlickers. After watching this movie, people's perspective about homosexuals would change and the result would be public hatred towards sexual minorities. I don't want to disrespect them but people will treat them like they are coming from another planet. They make fun of them or threaten them by revealing their sexual orientations. As I mentioned before, relationship between the same sex is not allowed in Restricted land so, a homosexual person should keep his sexual orientation to himself if he wants to live and if he doesn't want to be satirised by the majority of people. The present system asked people to be as cruel as possible to other people who are different from the majority. The minority can't even complain of being marginalised by the system because the majority will not support them. The censorship of the reality of homosexuality distracted people and therefore they can't comprehend what the real picture of a homosexual or a bisexual person is.

There is a famous hangout for these people where they are gathering together and talking. I have never gone there but I will. One of my friends describes the atmosphere of this place to me. Unfortunately, she was mocking their styles and their behaviour. I did say nothing. But I feel sorry for them because almost no one is going to sympathise with them. They can't understand their feelings because they don't know how to react when they confront with a homosexual person. They are either laughing or ignoring them. Sexual minority are not the only victims of the censorship. Truth is the most important victim of the system. The policy of Restricted land is to reject what truth is when the totalitarian regime knows about the possibility of people's revolution. You might have heard about one of the important political movements in Restricted land which is known as Great Awaking of Restricted landian people. This political movement refers to the rise of the protesters who demanded the removal of Mr X who was the bootlicker of the Leader. He became our president with the help of voting fraud. When people realised what the truth is, they asked for the justice and wanted Mr Y to become their president but the policy of the regime in this situation was to suffocate the protesters because Mr Y was considered as person who could revealed all the censorships of the political system. So, the policy of the totalitarian regime was to ignore our demand and introduced Mr X as the winner of presidential election and many protesters were sentenced to death. Their crime was to demand for the truth and the justice but they were unable to achieve their goal. When the bases of our society are made up of lies and censorship, people who are fond of the truth will lose. You may now understand how a simple censorship can change the destiny of a nation. If the system tries to subjugate people, it means that the regime wants to hide the dark secrets of its policy. You can't see a person protests against the political system of Restricted land without being sentenced to death or life imprisonment. By letting them go, the system would make a huge mistake because they are able to open people's eyes towards the dishonesty and censorship of the regime. If the government didn't react to the killing of the homosexual boy by his brothers is that because there is a policy behind it. The government aims to naturalise such violence against sexual minority because the present system can't accept such disgrace. Being homosexual means disgrace; however, being a liar means humanity. Well, this country is different from other countries. Why do I always compare Restricted land with other countries? It is unintentional. I don't mean to criticise my ancestral country, please don't get me wrong. I just want to retell my understanding and my stories about this nation. Some people would attack me because of the content of my book, but I can't be an indifferent person towards the cruelty of the government, the censorship of the totalitarian regime, and the ignorance of the majority of people. There is another form of censorship which represents itself in books and movies. I am an in love with books and films. As a book worm or as a person I have to tell you that we should illegally downloads the books or movies we want to read and to watch without paying attention to the copy-right law. I have to apologise for this on the behalf of Restricted landian people but there is no other way to watch or read the masterpieces. The condition of books and novels are better than movies and series because there are a few bookstores in our country which are selling the English novels but you can't find all the novels from your list. The translation of fictional or historical books are available in Restricted land but the translator cannot be 100% loyal to the original text when his or her translation will be edited by an editor. He can lose his job if he translates love sense or swears. So, as long as he works in Restricted land, he must respect the law of translation of books for a Restricted landian person. In other words, he has to delete the inappropriate parts of the book and he must create a whole new book for his reader. He doesn't want to, but he should. This can be seen as a disrespect to the original text. The author of the book would never realise this, the readers of the translated book aren't going to understand it either but the system should feel sorry for such transgression. But when it comes to movie and series the situation is quite different. Because we do not access to Netflix and because we are deprived of watching foreign movies in our theatre, we can only download them from the illegal websites and forget about the copy-right law. Put yourself in our situation what will you do if you were us? When you are cinephile, then you will die for watching all the movies which are directed by Steven Spielberg, Martin Scorsese, Quentin Tarantino, James Cameron, and Francis Ford Coppola. This would be a shame if you haven't watched the Godfather's trilogy yet. We are not allowed to watched such beautiful movies and we are forced to watched the meaningless movies of Restricted landian directors. No one has everything but we have nothing in our country to be proud of. Comparing movies like *In the Name of the Father*, *V for Vendetta*, and *The Shawshank Redemption* with the nonsense of Restricted landian movies with plots and contents of betrayal of men and weakness of women shows how many steps we are far from the salvation of our cinema.

As human beings we are not even allowed to watch the movie or to read the novel we want. Because we are living in a modernised version of North Korea. At least, people in Restricted land can watch these movies on their phone or laptops without being sentenced to death. As far as I know, the penalty for watching Hollywood movies in North Korea is death. So, we have to appreciate the government's kindness for giving us such limited chances to watch forbidden movies in our homes illegally. What kind of danger can threaten the system if they let people watch *V for Vendetta* in the theatre? I know the answer to that question. It will definitely lead to people's revolt because this movie can be observed as a push for people. V is a representative of the protesters who are angry at their governments. V sacrifices himself for his ideal. He fights with the totalitarian regime which destroys people's lives. At the end of the movie, all people become a V. They become a freeman. This movie must be censored in our society. If people unite to become a V, then the whole country will change. Becoming a V is not easy. We have to be ready to sacrifice our lives for a same goal. Achieving the V-goal means fulfilling the dreams of 85 million people. If we had a V in each house, we would have a better life. Ceasefire doesn't work when always people have to give up on their interest and their desires. I just remember about what my favourite Philosopher says about people's consent to specific ideology. Antonio Gramsci describes the strategy of ruling over the inferior groups of the society and how the ruling class are deceiving people. Of course, Gramsci is talking about a capitalist society and the gap between the bourgeoisie and the working class but his statement is not that irrelevant to what I want to put in to words. According to Gramsci:

Every single one of their words and attitudes serves the bourgeoisie and the State, because it helps prevent the masses from getting a clear view in the deluge of events going on around them and from noticing the chains that the new preachers of liberty, reform and positive advances are preparing to clinch around their wrists (1994: 242).

Okay, I hope you got the point. Gramsci is my God. I remember when I read his books, I could feel his words. I don't want to confuse you by quoting him but I strongly suggest you to read his books. By reading his books, you will understand about the dark secrets of capitalist societies and their operations. In addition, he will give you an insight about how the gap between the working class and the bourgeoisie is established by the owners of the power. Well, the reason which I started writing this book is because Gramsci gave me a proper insight about how to find out what reality is. He spent his life in jail because of his ideal. He was a V for me. and I want to be a V and therefore I started writing about the issues of Restricted land. Like every other V who has the guts to satirise the lifestyle, the culture, and the policy of his country. Please, accept my apology if my language is simple and plain, and if my book is not a literary one. I am not a big fan of figures of speech. I think this is it. My mum calls me a traitor again…

Note 28
An Epilogue

I think the hardest part of my book is the epilogue. I didn't know how should I start and now I don't know how should I finish this book. I let my heart talk instead of me using my insight to write the last note. Life is hard but for some people is even harder. I don't complain about my situation because in my country there are some people who do not even have a pair of shoes. I always thank God for what I had and I have never disrespected God for what I hadn't because it was the government who didn't bring them to us. I don't blame God for the irresponsibility of our Leader and the government. People write their own destiny. If they give their consent to their oppressive society, it means they will accept what the oppressive society is going to do to them. Then, we have to call ourselves not a V but a C. I let you decide what C stands for. Only a V can bring down the oppressive government. Living in a totalitarian country means all of us are a C and we are accepting our fate as a C. V stands for vendetta which means a V's duty is to take revenge on the cruelty of a totalitarian regime. But, in opposition to V, a C's job is to sit and ask the wind decides instead of him. We had some Vs in our country but the government either sent them up for life imprisonment or killed them. To rise against an oppressive government is not easy at all and people should bear in mind that rising means dying. Every movement or every revolution in the history of different countries explains how did people win. Winning is derived from sacrificing. Blood for victory. There is no movement without people sacrificing themselves. They have an ideal so they will fight for it in order to achieve their dreams. Most of us, including myself, are afraid of the consequences of rising. I have parents, I have sister, I don't want to be the reason of their death. Many people are against Restricted land's ideology and its oppressive government, but they prefer to forget about it. So, out of 85 million people if only 50000 people rise, revolution will never happen. At least in Restricted land would never happen. We have to either rebel together for the same goal or sit together and let the totalitarian regime of Restricted land suffocate us. If I talked about the disadvantages of being a citizen in Restricted land is because I wonder why people are so careless about their lives. I am not talking about those people who are rich enough not to care about what is happening around them. I am not talking about those people who want to emigrate. I am talking about the majority of people who are coming from the working class or the middle class who are experiencing an excruciating life. I am not in a position to judge them by asking why they aren't rising against the oppressive society of Restricted land but I am saying that we all have to do something about this inhuman society. Why we have to be Cs when we are capable of being Vs? This is all I want to ask from us. What prevent us from rising against the government which is itself standing against its people. Every four years, the candidates for presidential election promise that if they become president, they will eradicate inflation and they will bring freedom and happiness back to the society, but they won't.

The only thing I can see is that we are all suffering from soaring inflation and lack of happiness and freedom. Maybe the criteria of a president for measuring inflation, happiness, and freedom are different from ours. Maybe when a president in Restricted land says that he is going to take care of people's freedom and happiness, he means that he will control us like a master and won't let us be happy. It is our fault because we misunderstood him. His ambiguous speech distracted us. As a 26-year-old girl I have to confess that dealing with all those issues needs an infinite patience and power. I have none of them. I want to flee. I am tired. How many years a person can live. I have wasted the best years of my life in a country in which I couldn't even do girly stuff. I told my mother the other day about my feelings, about living in an oppressive society. 'I feel exhausted. I feel like a person who is waiting for her death. I am tired of waiting for a miracle. I want to go. This country is not my type. Hahaha… I want to live with respect,' I told her. 'Everywhere you go, people of that country will call you a stranger, a foreigner,' she said. 'Being a stranger in other countries is more acceptable than feeling like a foreigner in my hometown,' I said. 'What is your problem. You have a room of yours, you have never been hungry, you have never had a financial problem to buy clothes or stuff. What's wrong with you then? There are many people in this country that are hand-to-mouth,' she said. 'I know that and I thank God for what I have. But my problem is something else. Have you ever felt your soul is older than you? This is how I feel.'

‘I have MA in English literature. I worked hard for it and you know that. But is there any job for me? You know how much money an English teacher would earn? She can’t buy a car, she can’t buy a house, she can’t rent a house, she can’t even buy a plane ticket, she can’t have a dependent life of her own,’ I said. And it was the end of the conversation. It is a shame that I am still borrowing money from my parents. But many university students are doing it. There is no job for us. Educating is not free for us either. If there is a job for a student, the payment is awful so you will be dependent on your parents’ pockets for the rest of your life. I don’t want to write a long epilogue. Let me finish it here. Restricted land was never my enemy. I love my hometown. I love my country. I love the people. I had to write this book. Somebody should. I just pray for a better society in which the wolves go away and owls take control of the society. Bye for now. Maybe 10 years later, I’ll be back, writing about the utopian society of Free land.